A Lame Dog's Diary

S. Macnaughtan

Contents

A LAME DOG'S DIARY

BY

S. Macnaughtan

A LAME DOG'S DIARY

The Fern Cottage furniture was removed in a van to Fairview, as the new house is called—the handsomer pieces placed upon the outside of the van, and the commoner and least creditable of the bedroom furniture within. Everyone was at his or her window on the day that the Miss Traceys' furniture, with the best cabinet and the inlaid card-table duly displayed, was driven in state by the driver of the station omnibus through the town. A rumour got abroad that even more beautiful things were concealed from view inside the van, and the Miss Traceys satisfied their consciences by saying: 'We did not spread the rumour and we shall not contradict it.'

But the mystery concerns the furniture in quite a secondary sort of way, and it is only important as being the means of giving rise to the much discussed rumour in the town. For mark, the drawing-room furniture was taken at once and stored in a spare bedroom, and the drawing-room was left unfurnished. This fact might have remained in obscurity, for in winter time at least, it is not unusual for ladies to receive guests in the dining-room, with an apology for the drawing-room being a cold sitting-room during the frost. But Mrs. Lovekin, the lady who acts as co-hostess at every entertainment in our neighbourhood, handing about her friends' cakes and tea, and taking, we are inclined to think, too much upon herself, did, in a moment of expansion, offer to show the Traceys' house to the Blinds who happened to call there on the day when she was paying her respects to Miss Tracey. Mrs. Lovekin always removes her bonnet and cloak in every house, and this helps the suggestion that she is in some sort a hostess everywhere.

Palestrina, who was also calling on the Miss Traceys, gave me a full, true, and particular account of the affair the same evening.

'Mind the wet paint,' Mrs. Lovekin called from the dining-room window to the Miss Blinds as they came in at the gate, 'and I'll open the door." she remarked, as she sailed out into the passage to greet the sisters. Miss Ruby Tracey would rather have done this politeness herself, in order that she might hear the flattering remarks which people were wont to make about the hall paper. It is so well known that she and her sister keep three servants that they never have any hesitation in going to the door themselves. Whereas the Miss Blinds, who have only one domestic, would seem hardly to know where their front door is situated.

'What an elegant paper!' exclaimed Miss Lydia Blind, stopping awestruck in the little hall. Miss Lydia would, one knows, have something kind to say if she went to pay a call at a Kaffir hut.

'Yes,' said Mrs. Lovekin, in a proprietary sort of way; 'it is one of Moseley's which Smithson got down in his book of patterns. The blue paint is what they call "eggshell"—quite a new shade. Come this way and have a cup of tea.'

'I am sure it is all very simple,' said Miss Tracey, in a disparaging manner that showed her good breeding, as they sat down in the dining-room. 'How do you like the new carpet, Miss Belinda?'

'Glory, glory, glory!' said Miss Belinda; 'glory, glory, glory!'

'Show Miss Lydia the new footstools, Ruby dear,' said Miss Tracey, 'I am sure she would like to see them.' For we all believe—or like to believe—that to praise our property must be Miss Lydia's highest pleasure.

Mrs. Lovekin seized the opportunity to act as tea-maker to the party. She poured cream and sugar into the cups, with the remark that there was no one in Stowel whose tastes in these respects she did not know, and she handed a plate of cake to Miss Belinda, saying:

'There, my dear, you sit comfortable and eat that.'

'Glory, glory, glory!' said Miss Belinda.

The Miss Traceys had tea dispensed to them by the same hand, and accepted it with that slight sense of bewilderment which Mrs. Lovekin sometimes makes us feel when she looks after us in our own houses, and Miss Lydia Blind distributed her thanks equally between her and the Miss Traceys.,

Nothing was talked of that afternoon but the new house—its sunny aspect and its roomy cupboards in particular commanding the heartiest commendation. Presently the ladies were taken to see all over it, with the exception of one of the spare bedrooms and the drawing-room. They knew these rooms existed, because Miss

Tracey paused at the door of each, and said lightly, 'This is the drawing-room,' and 'This is another spare bedroom,' and although, as my sister confided to me, they would have given much to see the interior of the rooms, they could not do so, of course, uninvited.

They paused to admire something at every turn, even saying generously, but playfully, that there were many of Miss Tracey's possessions which they positively coveted for themselves. The Miss Traceys smilingly repudiated their felicitations, while Mrs. Lovekin accepted them and announced the price of everything. She become quite breathless, hurrying upstairs, while she exhibited stair-rods and carpets, and with shortened breath apostrophized them as being 'real brass' or 'the best Brussels at five-and-threepence.' No one is vulgar in Stowel, but Mrs. Lovekin is, we fear, not genteel.

At the close of the visit, Mrs. Lovekin again ushered the visitors into the hall, and opening, 'by the merest accident,' as she afterwards said—without, however, gaining any credence for her statement—opening by the merest accident the door of the drawing-room, she peeped in.

The drawing-room was void of furniture. The wild thought came into Mrs. Lovekin's mind—had the Traceys overbuilt themselves, and had the furniture, which had been carried so proudly through the town on the top of the furniture-van, been sold to pay expenses? The suggestion was immediately put aside. The Miss Traceys' comfortable means were so well known that such an explanation could not be seriously contemplated for a moment. No; putting two and two together, a closed spare bedroom and an empty drawing-room, and bringing a woman's instinct to bear upon the question, it all pointed to one thing—the Miss Traceys were going to give a party, probably an evening party, in honour of the new house, and the drawing-room furniture was being stored for safety in the spare bedroom until the rout was over.

Doubtless the first rumour of the Miss Traceys' party was meanly come by, but it was none the less engrossing, all the same. Miss Lydia hoped that no one would believe for a moment that she was in any way connected with the fraudulent intrusion that had been made into Miss Tracey's secret, and Miss Tracey said:

'I have known Mary Anne Lovekin for thirty years'—this was understating the case, but numbers are not exactly stated as we grow older—'but I never would have believed that she could have done such a thing.'

'Bad butter,' said Miss Belinda, shaking her head in an emphatic fashion; 'bad butter, bad butter!'

'I do not want to judge people,' said Miss Tracey, 'but there was a want of delicacy about opening a closed door which I for one cannot forgive.' The Miss Traceys' good-breeding is proverbial in Stowel, and it was felt that her uncompromising attitude could not but be excused when it was a matter of her most honourable sensibilities having been outraged.

'*I* shall not say what I think,' said Miss Ruby.

We often find that when Miss Ruby cannot transcend what her sister has said, she has a way of hinting darkly at some possible brilliance of utterance which for some reason she refrains from making.

'Bad butter!' said Miss Belinda; 'bad, bad, butter!'

Many years ago Miss Belinda Blind, who was then a beautiful young woman, was thrown from a pony carriage. The result of the fall was an injury to the spine, and she was smitten with a paralytic stroke which deprived her of all power of speech. She was dumb for some years, and then two phrases came back to her stammering tongue, 'glory' and 'bad butter.' She understands perfectly what is said to her, but she has no means of replying, save in this very limited vocabulary. And, strangely enough, these words can only be made to correspond with Miss Belinda's feelings. However polite her intentions may be, if at heart she disapproves she can only utter her two words of opprobrium. When a sermon displeases her, she sits in her pew muttering softly, and her lips show by their movement the words she is repeating, while a particularly good cup of tea will evoke from her the extravagant phrase, 'Glory, glory, glory!'

'Certainly,' I said to Miss Lydia, on the day succeeding the famous visit to the Traceys,' Mrs. Love-kin's information, if so it may be called, has been wrongly come by, and yet so frail is human nature one cannot help speculating upon it.'

'That is what is so sad,' said Miss Lydia; 'one almost feels as though sharing in Mrs. Lovekin's deceit by dwelling upon her information, and yet one's mind seems incapable of even partially forgetting such an announcement.'

Perhaps some suggestion of what was forming the topic of conversation in the town may have reached the Miss Traceys, and hastened their disclosure of the mystery. For very shortly afterwards, one morning when a flood of April sunshine had called us out of doors to wander on the damp paths of the garden, and watch bursting buds and listen to the song of birds in a very rural and delightful fashion, we were informed by a servant who tripped out in a white cap and apron, quite dazzling in the sunshine, that the Miss Traceys were within.

I appealed to my sister to furnish me with a means of escape. But she replied: 'I am afraid they have seen you. Besides, you know I like you to see people.' We went indoors, and Miss Ruby apologized for the untimely hour at which she and her sister had come, but explained it by saying, 'We wanted to find you alone.' And then we knew that the mystery was about to be solved.

'You are the first to hear about it,' said Miss Tracey, in a manner which was distinctly flattering. The Miss Traceys always sit very erect on their chairs, and when they come to call I always apologize for having my leg up on the sofa.

'The fact is,' Miss Tracey went on, 'that we knew that we could rely upon your good sense and judgment in a matter which is exercising us very seriously at present.'

'It is a delicate subject, of course,' said Miss Ruby, 'but one which we feel certain we may confide to you.'

'We always look upon Mr. Hugo as a man of the world,' said Miss Tracey, although he is such an invalid, and we rely upon the sound judgment of you both.'

Well, to state the subject without further preamble—but of course it must be understood that everything spoken this morning was to be in strict confidence—would we consider that they, the Miss Traceys, were sufficiently chaperoned if their brother the Vicar were present at the dance, and promised not to leave until the last gentleman had quitted the house?

I do not like to overstate a lady's age, and it is with the utmost diffidence that I suggest that Miss Ruby Tracy, the younger of the two sisters, may be on the other side of forty.

'You see, we have not only our own good name to consider,' said. Miss Tracey, 'but the memory of our dear and ever-respected father must, we feel, be our guide in this matter, and we cannot decide how he would have wished us to act. If our brother were married it would simplify matters very much.'

'You would have had your invitation before now,' said Miss Ruby, 'if we had been able to come to a decision, but without advice we felt that was impossible. I am sure,' she went on, giving her mantle a little nervous composing touch, and glancing aside, as though hardly liking to face any eye directly, 'I am sure the things one hears of unmarried women doing nowadays . . . but of course one would not like to be classed with that sort of person.'

Palestrina was the first of us who spoke.

'I think,' she said gravely, 'that as you are so well known here, nothing could be said.'

'You really think so?' said Miss Ruby.

But Miss Tracey still demurred. She said: 'But it is the fact of our being so well known here that really constitutes my chief uneasiness. We often feel,' she added with a sigh, 'that in another place we could have more liberty,'

'I assure you,' said Miss Ruby, in a tone of playful confession, 'that when we go to visit our cousins in London we are really quite shockingly frivolous, I do not know what it is about London; one always seems to throw off all restraint.'

'I think you are giving a wrong impression, dear,' said Miss Tracy. 'There was nothing in the whole of our conduct in London which would not bear repetition in Stowel, Only, in a place like this, one feels one must often explain one's actions, lest they should give rise to misrepresentations, whereas in London, although behaving I hope in a manner just as circumspect, one feels that no apology or explanation is needed.'

'There is a sort of cheerful privacy about London,' said the other sister,' which I find it hard to explain, but which is nevertheless enjoyable.'

To say that there is a dull publicity about the country, was too obvious a retort.

'I think we went out every evening when we were in West Kensington,' said Miss Tracey.

'Counting church in the evening,' said Miss Ruby.

'Still, those evening services in London almost count as going out,' said Miss Tracey; 'I mean, they are so lively, I often blame myself for not being able to look upon them more in the light of a religious exercise. I find it as difficult to worship in a strange pew as to sleep comfortably in a strange bed.'

The Miss Traceys' morning call lasted until one o'clock, and even then, as they themselves said, rising and shaking out their poplin skirts, there was much left un-discussed which they would still like to have talked over with us. The ball supper, as they called it, was to be cooked at home, and to consist of nothing which could not be 'eaten in the hand.'

Claret-cup was, to use Miss Tracey's own figure of speech, to be 'flowing' the whole evening, both in the dining-room with the sandwiches and cakes, and on a tray placed on a recess behind the ball door.

'Gentlemen always seem so thirsty,' said Miss Tracey, making the remark as though speaking of some animal of strange habits which she had considered with the bars of its cage securely fixed between herself and it at the Zoo.

'We have bought six bottles of Essence of Claret-cup,' said the younger sister, 'which we have seen very highly recommended in advertisements; and although it says that three tablespoonfuls will make a quart of the cup, we thought of putting four and so having it good.'

'As regards the music,' went on Miss Tracey, 'we have come, I think, to a very happy decision. A friend of ours knows a blind man who plays the piano for dances, and by employing him we feel that we shall be giving remunerative work to a very deserving person, as well as ensuring for ourselves a really choice selection of the most fashionable waltzes. Ruby pronounces the floor perfect,' said Miss Tracey, glancing admiringly at her younger sister's still neat figure and nimble feet; 'she has been practising upon it several times—'

'With the blinds down, dear,' amended Miss Ruby, simpering a little. 'We un-derstand,' she continued, 'that some chalk sprinkled over the boards before dancing begins is beneficial. You should have known Stowel in the old days, when there was a county ball every winter at the Three Jolly Post-boys—such a name!' continued Miss Ruby, who was in that curiously excited state when smiles and even giggles come easily.

'Now remember,' said Miss Tracey to Palestrina, as she took leave of her, 'you must come and help with the decorations on the morning of the dance. You can rest in the afternoon, so as to look your best and rosiest in the evening.'

In Stowel it is ingenuously admitted that a young lady should try and look her best when gentlemen are to be present, and rosy cheeks are still in vogue.

The Miss Traceys' drawing-room is not a very large room, even when empty of furniture, but it certainly had a most festive appearance when we drove up to the famous house-warming. Every curtain was looped up with evergreens, and every fireplace was piled with ivy, while two large flags, which were referred to several times as 'a display of bunting,' festooned the little staircase. Several friends in the village had lent their white-capped maids for the occasion, and these ran against each other in the little linoleum passage in a state of great excitement, and called each other 'dear' in an exuberance of affection which relieved their fluttered feelings.

A palm had been ordered from London and placed triumphantly in a corner—the palm had been kept as a surprise for us all. In the course of the evening it was quite a common thing to hear some girl ask her partner if he had seen The Palm, and if the reply was in the negative, the couple made a journey to the hall to look at it.

And here I must note a curious trait in the conversation prevalent in our select circle at Stowel. We all speak in capitals. The definite article is generally preferred to the 'a' or 'an' which points out a common noun, and so infectious is the habit, that when writing, for instance, of the Jamiesons, I find myself referring to The Family, with a capital, quite in a royal way, so perspicuously are capital letters suggested by their manner of speech. In the same way, the Taylors' uncle is never referred to by any of us except as The Uncle, and I feel sure that I should be doing the Traceys' plant an injustice, if I did not write it down The Palm.

This, however, is a digression.

The calmness of the Miss Traceys was almost overdone. They stood at the door of their drawing-room, each holding a small bouquet in her hand, and they greeted their guests as though nothing could be more natural than to give a dance, or to stand beneath a doorway draped with white lace curtains, and with a background of dissipated-looking polished boards and evergreens. The elder Miss Tracey, who is tall, was statuesque and dignified, the younger lady was conversational and natural almost to the point of artificiality—so determined was Miss Ruby to repudiate any hint of arrogance this evening. And it may be said of both sisters that they were strikingly well-bred and unembarrassed. Those who had seen them in all the flutter of preparations during the day—washing china and glass, issuing packets of candles from their store cupboard below the stairs, and jingling large bunches of keys—

could admire these outward symbols of ease, and appreciate the self-restraint that they involved.

I do not remember before, at any dance, seeing so many old young ladies, or so few and such very juvenile young men. The elderly young ladies smiled the whole time, while their boy partners looked preternaturally grave and solemn. They appeared to be shyly conscious of their shirt collars, which I fancy must have been made after some exaggerated pattern which I cannot now recall, but only remember that they appeared to be uncomfortably high and somewhat conspicuous, and that they gave one the idea of being the wearers' first high collars.

The Vicar, who had promised to come at eight o'clock, so that there should be no mistake about his being in the house from first to last of the dance, and who had been sent for in a panic at a quarter past eight, acted conscientiously throughout the entire entertainment. He began by inviting Mrs. Fielden to dance, and afterwards he asked every lady in turn according to her rank, and I do not think that during the entire evening his feet can have failed to respond to a single bar of the music. The blind musician was a little late in arriving, and we all sat round the drawing-room with our backs to the new blue wallpaper and longed for home. No one dared to offer to play a waltz, in case it should be considered an affront at a party where etiquette was so conspicuous, and where the peculiar Stowel air of mystery pervaded everything.

The Jamiesons arrived, a party of nine, in the station omnibus, and chatted in the hearty, unaffected manner peculiar to themselves, waving little fans to and fro in the chilly air of the new drawing-room, and putting an end to the solemn silence which had distinguished the first half-hour of the party. Each of the sisters wore a black dress relieved by a touch of colour, and carried a fan. Their bright eyes shone benignly behind their several pairs of pince-nez; and as they shook hands with an air of delight with every single person in the room when they entered, their arrival caused quite a pleasant stir.

Mrs. Lovekin had already, in her character of co-hostess, begun to distribute the Essence of Claret-cup that, diluted with water, formed the staple beverage of the evening and was placed on a small table behind the hall-door. There was rather a curious sediment left at the bottom of the glasses, and the flavour of cucumber suggested vaguely to one that the refreshment might be claret-cup. Very young men in split white kid gloves, drank a good deal of it.

At last the blind musician was led solemnly across the room, and took up his position at the piano. He always left off playing before a figure of a quadrille or lancers was finished, and then the dancers clapped their hands to make him continue, and the elderly young ladies smiled more than ever. At the second or third waltz my sister was in the proud position of being claimed in turn by the Vicar as his partner, and the position, besides being prominent, was such an enviable one that Palestrina, who is not more given to humility than other good-looking young women of her age, was carried away by popular feeling so far as to remark in a tone of gratitude that this was very kind of him.

He replied, 'I have made up my mind to sacrifice myself for one night;' and one realized that lofty positions and a prominent place in the world, may carry with them sufficient humiliations to keep one meek.

The conscientious Vicar did not allow his partner to sit down once throughout the entire waltz, and I think the blind musician played at greater length than usual. I began to wonder if her partner regarded my excellent Palestrina as a sort of Sandow exerciser, and whether he was trying to get some healthy gymnastics, if not amusement, out of their dance together.

'There!' he said at last, placing her on a chair beside me as a fulfilled duty; and, feeling that she was expected to say 'Thank you,' Palestrina meekly said it.

'I have only danced once in the last twenty years,' said the Vicar, 'and that was with some choir-boys.' And the next moment the blind man began to play again, and he was footing it with conscientious energy with Miss Lydia Blind.

Young ladies who had sat long with their empty programmes in their hands, now began to dance with each other, with an air of overdone merriment, protesting that they did not know how to act gentleman, but declaring with emphasis that it was just as amusing to dance with a girl-friend as with a man.

The music, as usual, failed before the end of each figure of the dance, and the curate, who wore a pair of very smart shoe-buckles, remarked to me that the lancers was a dance that created much di-version, and I replied that they were too amusing for anything.

The Jamiesons' youngest brother, who is in a shipping-office in London, had come down to Stowel especially for this occasion. Once, some years ago, Kennie, as he is called, made a voyage in one of the shipping company's large steamers to South America. He landed at Buenos Ayres, armed to the teeth, and walked about the pavement of that highly-civilized town, with its wooden pavements and plate-glass shop windows, in a sombrero and poncho, and with terrible weapons stuck in his belt. At the end of a week he returned in the same ship in which he had made the outward voyage, and since then he has had tales to tell of those wild regions with which any of the stories in the ***Boys' Own Paper*** are tame in comparison. In his dress and general appearance he even now suggests a pirate king. His tales of adventure are always accompanied by explanatory gestures and demonstrations, and it is not unusual to see Kennie stand up in the midst of an admiring circle of friends and make some fierce sabre-cuts in the air. He was dressed with a red cummerbund round his waist, and he drew attention to it by an apology to every one of his partners for having it on. 'One gets into the habit of dressing like this out there,' he said, in a tone of excuse. The Pirate Boy was in great demand at the dance.

Pretty Mrs. Fielden, who had driven over from Stanby, beautifully dressed as usual, and slightly amused, ordered her carriage early, and had merely come to oblige those quaint old dears, the Miss Traceys.

Even at the house-warming Mrs. Fielden would have considered it quite impossible to sit out a dance. She brought an elderly Colonel with her, and she conducted him into a corner behind The Palm and talked to him there till it was her turn to dance with the Vicar. Had it not been Mrs. Fielden, whose position placed her above criticism, the breath of envy might have whispered that it was hardly fair that one couple should occupy the favourite sitting-out place—two drawing-room chairs beneath The Palm—to the exclusion of others. But Mrs. Fielden being who she was, the young ladies of Stowel were content to pass and repass the coveted chairs, and to whisper admiringly, 'How exquisite she is looking to-night!'

'Is there anything of me left?' she said to me, looking cool and unruffled when her dance with the Vicar was over. She had only made one short turn of the room with him, and her beautiful dress and her hair were quite undisturbed.

'You haven't danced half so conscientiously as his other partners,' I said.

'I wanted to talk about the parish,' said Mrs. Fielden, 'so I stopped. I think I should like to go and get cool somewhere.'

'I will take you to sit under The Palm again, as Colonel Jardine did,' I replied,' and you shall laugh at all the broad backs and flat feet of our country neighbours, and hear everybody say as they pass how beautiful you are.'

Mrs. Fielden turned her head towards me as if to speak, and I had a sudden vivid conviction that she would have told me I was rude, had I not been a cripple with one leg.

We sat under The Palm. Mrs. Fielden never rushes into a conversation. Presently she said:

'Why do you come to this sort of thing? It can't amuse you.'

'You told me the other day,' I said, 'that I ought to cultivate a small mind and small interests.'

'Did I?' said Mrs. Fielden lightly. 'If I think one thing one day, I generally think quite differently a day or two after. To-night, for instance, I think it is a mistake for you to lean against the Miss Traceys' new blue walls and watch us dance.'

'I'm not sure that it isn't better than sitting at home and reading how well my old regiment is doing in South Africa. Besides, you know, I am writing a diary.'

'Are you?' said Mrs. Fielden.

'You advised it,' I said.

'Did I?'

When Mrs. Fielden is provoking she always looks ten times prettier than she does at other times.

'A good many people in this little place,' I said, 'have made up their minds to "do the work that's nearest" and to help "a lame dog over stiles." I think I should be rather a brute if I didn't respond to their good intentions.'

'I don't think they need invent stiles, though!' said Mrs. Fielden quickly, 'woodcarving, and beating brass, and playing the zither—'

'I do not play the zither,' I said.

'—are not stiles. They are making a sort of obstacle race of your life.'

'Since I have begun to write the diary,' I said, 'I've been able to excuse myself attempting these things, even when tools are kindly brought to me. And so far, no one has so absolutely forgotten that there is a lingering spark of manhood in me as to suggest that I should crochet or do cross-stitch.'

'You know I am going to help to write the diary,' said Mrs. Fielden, 'only I'm afraid I shall have to go to all their tea-parties, shan't I, to get copy?'

'You will certainly have to go,' I said.

'I'm dreadfully bored to-night, aren't you?' she said confidentially, and in a certain radiant fashion as distant as the Poles from boredom. 'No one can really enjoy this sort of thing, do you think? It's like being poor, or anything disagreeable of that sort. People think they ought to pretend to like it, but they don't.'

'I wish I could entertain you better,' I said sulkily; 'but I'm afraid I never was the least bit amusing.'

Mrs. Fielden relapsed into one of her odd little silences, and I determined I would not ask her what she was thinking about.

Presently Colonel Jardine joined us, and she said to him: 'Please see if you can get my carriage; it must be five o'clock in the morning at least.' And the next moment I was made to feel the egotism of imagining I had been punished, when she bade me a charming 'good-night.' She smiled congratulations on her hostesses on the success of the party, and pleaded the long drive to Stanby as an excuse for leaving early. The Colonel wrapped her in a long, beautiful cloak of some pale coloured velvet and fur—a sumptuous garment at which young ladies in shawls looked admiringly—and Mrs. Fielden slipped it on negligently, and got into her brougham.

'Oh, how tired I am!' she said.

'It was pretty deadly,' said the Colonel. 'Did you taste the claret-cup?' he added, making a grimace in the dark.

'Oh, I found it excellent,' said Mrs. Fielden quickly.

Margaret Jamieson now took her place at the piano to enable the blind man to go and have some supper, but having had it, he slept so peacefully that no one could bear to disturb him, so between them the young ladies shared his duties till the close of the evening.

Palestrina had suggested, as a little occupation for me, that I should write out programmes for the dance, and I had done so. Surely programmes were never so little needed before! Every grown man had left the assembly long before twelve o'clock struck, the feebleness of the excuses for departing thus early, being only equalled by the gravity with which they were made. Even the lawyer, who we thought would have remained faithful to the end, pleaded that since he ricked his knee, he is obliged to have plenty of rest. The Pirate Boy had had some bitter words with the lawyer at a previous stage in the evening, about the way in which the lancers should be danced, and had muttered darkly, 'I won't make a disturbance in a lady's house, but I have seen a fellow called out for less.' He considered that the lawyer was running away, unable to bear his cold, keen eye upon him during the next lancers, and he watched him depart, standing at the head of the tiny staircase beneath the display of bunting, with his arms folded in a Napoleonic attitude.

All good things come to an end, and even the Vicar of Stowel must have felt that there are limits to the most conscientious energy. And girls, dancing with each other, learned perhaps that the merriment caused by acting as a man is not altogether lasting; while elderly young ladies, although agreed in smiling to the very end, must be aware how fixed in expression such a smile may become towards the end of a long evening,

Good-nights were said, and carriages were called up with a good deal of unnecessary shouting, while the Pirate Boy insisted upon going to the heads of the least restive horses, and soothing them in a way which he said he had learned from those Gaucho fellows out there.

I have never been able to tell what the Miss Traceys thought about their dance. If they were disappointed, the world was not allowed to probe that tender spot. Possibly they were satisfied with its success; the proprietary instinct of admiration applies to entertainments as well as to tangible possessions. But that satisfaction, if it existed, was modestly veiled—the house-warming was less discussed by them than by anyone else. Miss Ruby spoke rather wistfully one day about simple pleasures being the best and safest after all, and she alluded, with a sigh, to the time which must come some day when she would be no longer young. Miss Tracey drew herself up and said: 'A woman is only as old as she looks, my dear,' and glanced admiringly at her sister.

The diluted Essence of Claret-cup was bottled, and formed a nice light luncheon wine at the Miss Traceys' for many weeks afterwards. The furniture was brought down from the spare bedroom by the maids, who walked the heavier pieces in front of them with a curious tip-toeing movement of the castors of the several easy chairs. The art tiles in the grate were cleared of their faded burden of evergreens, and The Palm was carried into the bay window where it could be seen from the road.

I drove over to see Mrs. Fielden and to ask her if she thought I had been a sulky brute at the dance.

'Were you?' said Mrs. Fielden, lifting her pretty dark eyebrows; 'I forget.'

CHAPTER II

PALESTRINA and I live in the country, and whenever we are dull or sad, like the sailors in Mr. Gilbert's poem, we decide that our neighbourhood is too deadly uninteresting, and then we go and see the Jamiesons. They are our nearest neighbours, as they are also amongst our greatest friends, and the walk to their house is a distance that I am able to manage. I believe that our visits to the Jamiesons are most often determined by the state of the weather. If we have passed a long wet day indoors, I feel that it is going to be a Jamieson day, and I know that my sister will say to me after tea, 'Suppose we go over and see the Jamiesons;' and she generally adds that it is much better than settling down for the evening at five o'clock in the afternoon.

I do not think that Palestrina was so sociable a young woman, nor did she see so much of her neighbours before I came home an invalid from South Africa—I got hit in the legs at Magersfontein, and had the left one taken off in the hospital at Wynberg—but she believes, no doubt rightly, that the variety that one gets by seeing one's fellow-men is good for a poor lame dog who lies on a sofa by the fire the greater part of the day, wishing he could grow another leg or feel fit again.

Acting upon this unalterable conviction of my sister, we drive about in the afternoon and see people, and they come and see me and suggest occupations for me. In Lent I had a more than usual number of callers, which says much for the piety of the place, as well as for the goodness of heart of its inhabitants.

There is a slight coolness between what is known as the 'County' and the Jamiesons, and their name is never mentioned without the accompanying piece of information, 'You know, old Jamieson married his cook!' To be more exact, Mrs. Jamieson was a small farmer's daughter, and Captain Jamieson fell in love with her when, having left the army, he went to learn practical farming at old Higgins's, and he loved her faithfully to the day of his death. She is a stout, elderly woman who speaks very little, but upon whom an immense amount of affection seems to be lavished by her family of five daughters and two sons. And it has sometimes seemed to my sister and me that her good qualities are of a lasting and passive sort, which exist in large measure in the hearts of those who bestow this boundless affection. Mrs. Jamieson's form of introducing herself to anyone she meets, consists in giving an account of the last illness and death of her husband. There is hardly a poultice which was placed upon that poor man which her friends have not heard about. And when she has finished, in her flat, sad voice, giving every detail of his last disorder, Mrs. Jamieson's conversation is at an end. She has learned, no doubt unconsciously, to gauge the characters of new acquaintances by the degree of interest which they evince in Captain Jamieson's demise. It is Mrs. Jamieson's test of their true worth.

Of the other sorrow which saddened a nature that perhaps was never very gay, Mrs. Jamieson rarely speaks. Possibly because she thinks of it more than of anything else in the world. Among her eight children there was only one who appeared to his mother to combine all perfection in himself. He was killed by an accident in his engineering works seven years ago, and although his friends will, perhaps, only remember him as a stout young fellow who sang sea songs with a distended chest, his mother buried her heart with him in his grave, and even the voice of strangers is lowered as they say, 'She lost a son once.'

The late Captain Jamieson, a kindly shrewd man and a Scotchman withal, was agent to Mrs. Fielden, widow of the late member for Stanby, and when he died, his income perished with him, and The Family of Jamieson—a large one, as has been told—were thankful enough to subsist on their mother's inheritance of some four or five hundred a year, bequeathed to her by the member of the non-illustrious house of Higgins, late farmer deceased. It is a hospitable house, for all its narrow means, and there live not, I believe, a warmer-hearted or more generous family than these good Jamiesons. The girls are energetic, bright and honest; their slender purses are at the disposal of every scoundrel in the parish, and their time, as well as their boundless energy, are devoted to the relief of suffering or to the betterment of mankind.

Mrs. Fielden is of the opinion that nothing gives one a more perfect feeling of rest than going to Belmont, as the Jamiesons' little house is called, and watching them work. She calls it the 'Rest Cure.' Every one of the five sisters, except Maud, who is the beauty of the family, wears spectacles, and behind these their bright, intelligent small eyes glint with kindness and brisk energy. The worst feature of this excellent family is their habit of all talking at the same time, in a certain emphatic fashion which renders it difficult to catch what each individual is saying, and this is especially the case when three of the sisters are driving sewing-machines simultaneously. They have a genius for buying remnants of woollen goods at a small price, and converting them into garments for the poor, and their first question often is, as they hold a piece of flannel or serge triune phantly aloft, 'What do you think I gave for that?' Palestrina always names at least twice the sum that has purchased the goods, and has thereby gained a character for being dreadfully extravagant but sympathetic.

'I do not believe,' I said to Palestrina the other day, 'that these good Jamiesons have a thought beyond making other people happy.'

'That and getting married are the sole objects of their existence,' said Palestrina.

'It is very odd,' I said, 'that women so devoid of what might be called sentiment are yet so bent upon this very thing.'

'Eliza told me to-day,' said Palestrina, 'that as Kate has not mentioned one single man in her letters home, they cannot help thinking that there is something in it.'

The Jamiesons have the same vigorous, energetic ideas about matrimony that they have about everything else, and almost their sole grievance, naively expressed, is that Maud, 'who gets them all'—meaning, I believe, offers of marriage—is the only one of the family who is unable to make up her mind clearly on this momentous question.

'We should not mind,' say the conclave of sisters during one of the numerous family discussions on this subject,' even if she does get all the admirers, for of course she is the pretty one, if only she would accept one of them. But she always gets undecided and silly as soon as they come to the point.'

It should be noted in passing that the different stages of development in love affairs are shrewdly noted and commented upon by the Jamiesons. The first evidence of a man's preference is that he 'is struck'; and the second, when he begins to visit at the house, is known as 'hovering.' An inquiry after Maud's health will sometimes elicit the unexpected reply that another admirer is hovering at present. The third stage is reached when the lover is said to be 'dangling,' and the final triumph, when

Maud has received a proposal, is noted as having 'come to the point.'

If Maud's triumphs are watched with small sighs of envy by her sisters, they are a source of nothing but gratification to them to retail to the outside world. There is a strict account kept of Maud's 'conquests' in the letters sent to relatives, and the evening's post will sometimes contain the startling announcement that Maud has had a fourth in one year.

'Of course, you know how fond we all are of each other,' said Eliza Jamieson to me one day with one of those unexpected confidences which the effeminacy of sickness seems to warrant, if not actually to invite, 'but we can't help thinking that, humanly speaking, we should all have a better chance if only Maud would marry. No one would wish her to marry without love, but we fear she is looking for perfection, and that she will never get, and it was really absurd of her to be so upset when she discovered, after nearly getting engaged to Mr. Reddy, that he wore a wig. After all, a man may be a good Christian in spite of having no hair.'

'That is undoubtedly a fact,' I said warmly.

'And Mr. Reddy had excellent prospects,' said Eliza, 'although perhaps nothing very tangible at present. Then there was Albert Gore, to whom one must admit Maud gave every encouragement, and we had begun to think it quite hopeful, but just at the end she discovered that she could not care for anyone called Albert, which was too silly.'

'She might have called him Bertie,' I suggested.

'Yes,' said Eliza eagerly; 'and you see, none of us hope or expect to marry a man who has not some of these little drawbacks, so I really do not see why Maud should expect it.'

Five matrimonial alliances in one family are, perhaps, not easily arranged for in a quiet country neighbourhood, yet there is always a hopeful tone about these family discussions, and it is very common to hear the Miss Jamiesons relate at length what they intend to do when they are married.

And there is yet another maiden to be arranged for in the little house; Mettie is the Jamieson's cousin who lives with them, and I believe that what appeals to me most strongly in this unknown provincial family, is their kindness to the little shrunken, tiresome cousin who shares their home. Mettie is like some strange little bright bird, utterly devoid of intelligence, and yet with the alertness of a sparrow.

Her beady eyes are a-twinkle in a restless sort of way all day long, and her large thin nose has always the appearance of having the skin stretched unpleasantly tightly across it. The good Jamiesons never seem to be ruffled by her presence among them, and this forbearance certainly commands one's respect. Mettie travesties the Jamiesons in every particular. She has adopted their matrimonial views with interest, and she utters little platitudes upon the subject with quite a surprising air of sapience. One avoids being left alone with Mettie whenever it is possible to do so, for, gentle creature though she is, her remarks are so singularly devoid of interest that one is often puzzled to understand why they are made. Yet I see one or other of the Jamiesons walk to the village with her every day—her little steps pattering beside their giant strides, while the bird-like tongue chirps gaily all the way.

Everyone in our little neighbourhood walks into the village every day; it is our daily dissipation; and frivolous persons have been known to go twice or three times. On days when Palestrina thinks that I am getting moped, she steals the contents of my tobacco-jar, and then says, without blushing, that she has discovered that my tobacco is all finished, and that we had better walk into the village together and get some more. When I am in a grumpy mood, I reply: 'It's all right, thank you, I have plenty upstairs.' But it generally ends in my taking the walk with my sister.

Our house is pleasantly situated where, by peeping through a tangle of shrubs and trees, we can see the lazy traffic of the high-road that leads to the village. Strangers pause outside the screen of evergreens sometimes and peep between the branches to see the quaint gables of the old house. Its walls have turned to a soft yellow colour with old age, and its beams are of oak, gray with exposure to the storms of many winters.

'This old hall of yours is much too dark,' Mrs. Fielden said, when she came to call the other day muffled up in velvet and fur. She lighted the dull afternoon by something that is radiant and holiday like about her, and left us envying her for being so pretty and so young and gay. 'Oh, I know,' she said in her whimsical way, 'that it is Jacobean and early Tudor and all sorts of delightful things, but it isn't very cheerful, you know. I'm so glad it is near the road; I think if I built a house I should like it to be in Mansion House Square, or inside a railway-station. Don't you love spending a night at a station hotel? I always ask for a room overlooking the platform, for I like the feeling of having the trains running past me all night. I love your house really,' she said, 'only I'm afraid it preaches peace and resignation, and all those things which I consider so wrong.'

Since I have been laid up I have been recommended to carve wood, to beat brass, to stuff sofa-cushions, and to play the zither; but these things do not amuse me much. It was Mrs. Fielden who suggested that I should write a diary.

'You must grumble,' she said, raising her pretty eyebrows in the affected way she has. 'It wouldn't be human if you didn't; so why not write a diary, and have a real good grumble on paper every night before you go to bed. Of course, if I were in your place I should grumble all day instead, and go to sleep at night. But I'm not the least bit a resigned person. If anything hurts me I scream at once; and if there is anything I don't like doing I leave it alone. Palestrina,' she said to my sister, 'don't let him be patient; it's so bad for him.'

Palestrina smiled, and said she was afraid it was very dull for me sometimes.

'But if one is impatient enough, one can't be dull,' said Mrs. Fielden. 'It's like being cross—'

'I am constitutionally dull,' I said. 'I used to be known as the dullest man in my regiment.'

'You studied philosophy, didn't you?' said Mrs. Fielden. 'That must be so depressing.'

I was much struck by this suggestion. 'I dare say you are quite right,' I said, 'although I had not seen it in that light before. But I'm afraid it has not made me very patient, nor given me a great mind.'

'Of course, what you want just now,' said Mrs. Fielden gravely, 'is a little mind. You must lie here on your sofa, and take a vivid interest in what all the old ladies say when they come to call on Palestrina. And you must know the price of Mrs. Taylor's last new hat, and how much the Traceys spend on their washing-bill, and you must put it all down in your diary. I'll come over and help you sometimes, and write all the wicked bits for you, only I'm afraid no one ever is wicked down here.'

'Good-bye,' she said, holding out the smallest, prettiest, most useless-looking little hand in the world. 'And please,' she added earnestly, 'get all this oak painted white, and hang some nice muslin curtains in the windows.'

Kindly folk in Stowel are always ingenuously surprised at anyone caring to live in the country; and although it is but a mile from here to the vestry hall, and much less by the fields, they often question us whether we do not feel lonely at nighttime, and they are of the opinion that we should be better in 'town.' They frequently speak of going into the country for change of air or on Bank Holidays; but considering that the last house in the village—and, like the City of Zoar, it is but a little one—is built amongst fields, it might be imagined that these rural retreats could readily be found without the trouble of hiring the four-wheeled dog-cart from the inn, or of taking a journey by train. Yet an expedition into the country is often talked of as being a change, and friends and relations living outside the town are considered a little bit behindhand in their views of things—'old-feshioned' they call it in Stowel—and these country cousins are visited with just a touch of kindly condescension by the dwellers in a flower-bordered, tree-shadowed High Street.

One is brought rather quaintly into immediate correspondence with the domestic concerns of everyone in Stowel, and Palestrina has been coaching me in the etiquette of the place. It is hardly correct to do any shopping at dinner-time, when the lady of the house, busy feeding her family, has to be called from the inner parlour, where that family may all be distinctly seen from the shop. Driving or walking through Stowel at the hour thus consecrated by universal consent to gastronomy, one might almost imagine it to be a deserted village. Even the dogs have gone inside to get a bone; and one says, as one walks down the empty streets, 'Stowel dines.'

When a shop is closed on Thursday, which is early closing day, one can generally 'be obliged' by ringing at the house-bell, and under conduct of the master of the place, may enter the darkened shop by the side-door, and be accommodated with the purchase that one requires. For the old custom still holds of living—where it seems most natural for a merchant to live—in the place where he does his business. There is a pleasurable feeling of excitement even in the purchase of a pot of Aspinall's enamel behind closed shutters, and this is mingled with a feeling of solemnity and privilege, which I can only compare in its mixed effect upon me, to going behind the scenes of a theatre, or to being permitted to enter the vestry of a church.

Any purchases, except those which may be called necessaries, are seldom indulged in in our little town. A shop which contains anything but dress and provisions has few customers, and its merchandise becomes household fixtures. I called at the furniture shop the other day; the place looked bare and unfamiliar to me, but

I did not realize what was amiss until my sister exclaimed, 'Where is the sofa?' The sofa had been for sale for fifteen years, and had at last been purchased. There are other things in the shop which I think must have been there much longer, and I believe their owner would part with them with regret, even were a very fair profit to be obtained for them. Palestrina tells me she ordered some fish the other day, and was met with the objection that 'I fear that piece will be too big for your fish-kettle, ma'am,' although she had never suspected that the size of her fish-kettle was a matter that was known to the outside world.

And yet Stowel prides itself more upon its reserve than upon anything else, except perhaps its gentility. There is a distinct air of mystery over any and every one of the smallest affairs of daily life in the little place, and I hardly think that our neighbours would really enjoy anything if it were 'spoken about' before the proper time. There is something of secrecy in the very air of the town. No one, I am told, has ever been known to mention, even casually, what he or she intends to have for dinner; and the butcher has been warned against calling across the shop to the lady at the desk 'Two pounds of rump-steak for Miss Tracey,' or 'One sirloin, twelve two, for the Hall.' Mr. Tomsett, who was the first butcher to introduce New Zealand mutton to the inhabitants of Stowel, lost his custom by this vulgar habit of assorting his joints in public. And Miss Tracey, who knew him best (he was still something of a stranger, having been in Stowel only five years), warned him that that was not the sort of thing we were accustomed to. 'If you must make our private concerns public in this way,' she said, 'at least it cannot be necessary to mention in what country the mutton was raised.'

It is even considered a little indelicate to remain in the post-office when a telegram is being handed in. And parcels addressed and laid on the counter at the grocer's, although provocative of interest, are not even glanced at by the best people.

On the authority of my sister, I learn that when the ladies of Stowel do a little dusting in the morning the front blinds are pulled down. And keen though the speculation may be as to the extent of our neighbours' incomes, the subject is, of course, a forbidden one. Poor though some of these neighbours are, a very kindly charity prevails in the little town. When the elder Miss Blind was ill—as she very often is, poor thing!—it might seem a matter of coincidence to the uninitiated that during that week everyone of her friends happened to make a little strong soup, a portion of which was sent to the invalid—just in case she might fancy it; while the Miss Traceys, who, as all the world knew, had inherited a little wine from their father, the late Vicar of the parish, sent their solitary remaining bottle of champagne, with their compliments, to Miss Belinda. The champagne proved flat after many a year of storage in the lower cupboard of Miss Tracey's pantry, but the two sisters to whom it was sent, not being familiar with the wine, did not detect its faults, and they left, the green bottle with the gilt neck casually standing about for weeks afterwards, from an innocent desire to impress their neighbours with its magnificence.

Palestrina, with the good intention I believe, of providing me with what she calls an object for a walk, asked me to call and inquire for Miss Blind on the day that the bottle of champagne was drawn and sampled. Miss Lydia was in the sick-room, and Mrs. Lovekin, who had called to inquire, was sitting in the little parlour when I entered. 'How do you do?' she said. 'I suppose you have heard about Belinda and the champagne?'

The reproachful note in Mrs. Lovekin's voice, which seemed to tax the invalid with ingratitude, subtly conveyed the impression that the flat champagne had not agreed with poor Miss Belinda.

CHAPTER III

IT is a subject of burning curiosity with every woman in Stowel, to know whether it is a fact that the Taylors have taken to having late dinner instead of supper since Mrs. Taylor's uncle was made a K.C.B. There was something in a remark which Miss Frances Taylor made which distinctly suggested that such a change had been effected, but Stowel, on the whole, is inclined to discredit the rumour. A portrait of the General has been made in London, from a photograph in uniform which Mrs. Taylor has of him, and it has been framed, regardless of expense, by the photographer in the High Street. Mr. Taylor had at one time thought of having the whole thing done in London, but it had been decided by an overwhelming majority that it would be only fair to give the commission to provide the frame to someone in our own town; and Mr. and Mrs. Taylor have given a permission, which amounts to a command, that the portrait of 'Sir John' shall be placed in the window for a week before it is sent home, so that Stowel may see it—for the Taylors, it should be remembered, do not receive everyone at their own house.

To-day I met the younger Miss Blind—Miss Lydia, she is generally called—at the window of the photographer's, to which she had made a pilgrimage, as we all intended to do, to see the famous picture. Probably she had stood there for some time, for she turned nervously towards me, and said in a tone of apology and with something of an effort in her speech: 'I used to know him.'

'Ah!' I replied. 'I suppose he has often been down to stay with the Taylors?'

'He has not been once in twenty years,' said Lydia.

I was thinking of other things, and I do not know why it suddenly struck me that there was a tone of regret, even of hopelessness, in Miss Lydia's voice, and that she spoke as one speaks, perhaps, when one has waited long for something.

Lydia Blind is a tall woman with a slight, stooping figure. Sometimes I have wondered if it is only her sister's constant ill-health that has made Miss Lydia stoop a little. There is something delicately precise about her, if so gentle a woman can fitly be described as precise. Perhaps her voice explains her best, as a woman's voice will often do; it is low and of a very charming quality, although broken now and then by asthma. Each word has its proper spacing, and does not intrude upon the next; each vowel possesses the rare characteristic of its proper sound. I have never heard her use an out-of-the-way expression; but her simple way of speaking has an old-fashioned gracefulness about it, and her manner, with all its simplicity, is digni-fied by reason of its perfect sincerity. Her eyes are large and gray, and set somewhat far apart; her hair is worn in a fringe so demure and smooth, so primly curled, that it has the appearance of plainly-brushed hair. It is Mrs. Fielden who says that no good woman can do her hair properly, and she wonders if St. Paul's recommendations as to plain braids has for ever stamped the hairdresser's profession as a dangerous art.

To-day when I met Lydia it struck me suddenly to wonder how old she was. Perhaps something in the insolent youthfulness of the spring-time suggested the thought, or it may have been because Miss Lydia looked tired.

When one meets a friend in Stowel High Street, it is considered very cold be-haviour merely to bow to them. We not only stop and chat for a few minutes, but it is the friendly fashion of the place for ladies to say to each other, 'Which way are you going? and to accompany their friend a little way along the sunny, uneven pavement, while offers to come in and rest are generally given and accepted at the end of the promenade. Of course it is quite unusual for gentlemen to be detained in this way, and I am sure it cost Miss Lydia an effort to suggest to me that I should come in and sit down for a little while, and that she only did so because I seemed tired. Also, I think that a man with a crutch and with but one leg—and that one not very sound—is not considered such a source of danger to ladies living alone as a strong and hale man is supposed to be. We stopped at the little green gate in the village street, with its red flagged pathway beyond, bordered with spring-flowers— wall-flowers, early blooming in this warm and sheltered corner, forget-me-nots and primroses, while a brave yellow jasmine starred with golden flowers covered the walls of the cottage. I asked after her sister's health, and Miss Lydia begged me to come in and rest for a few minutes, which I did, for I was horribly tired. But this was one of Miss Belinda's bad days, and her sister, who watches every variation in colour in the hollow cheeks and deep-set eyes of the invalid, saw that she was un- able to speak, and motioned me out of the room. She showed me into her own little sanctum and gave me a cushioned chair by the window and said: 'Do wait for a few minutes and rest. I can see that my sister wants to say something to me, but she is always more than usually inarticulate when she is in one of these nervous states.'

I have been thinking a good deal about old maids lately—one has time to think about all manner of subjects when one is lying down most of the day. Mrs. Fielden is of opinion that an old maid may have an exaggerated sense of humour. To my mind her danger may be that she is always rather pathetically satisfied with every- thing. She prefers the front seat of a carriage and the back-seat of a dog-cart, and the leg of a chicken and a tiny bedroom. Doubtless this is a form of self-respect. This suitability of tastes on the part of an old maid enables her to say, as she does with almost suspicious frequency, that she gets dreadfully spoiled wherever she goes. Adaptability to environment is the first law of existence, and yet there may have been times, even in the life of an old maid, when she has yearned for the wing of a chicken.

The little room into which Miss Lydia ushered me was plainly furnished, but Miss Lydia says that she is always getting something pretty given to her to add to her treasures. Her room is, indeed, rather suggestive of a stationer's shop window, where a card with 'Fancy goods in great variety' is placed. It would not be unkind

to hint of some of the articles on the table and on the wall-brackets, that they must
have been purchased more as a kindly remembrance at Christmas-time or on birth-
days, than from any apparent usefulness to the recipient. There are three twine-cas-
es, from which the scissors have long since been abstracted by unknown dishonest
persons; and there are four ornamental thermometers, each showing its own fixed
and unalterable idea respecting the temperature of the room. A large number of unframed sketches, which children have given her, are fastened to the wall by pins, or
hung on tacks whose uncertain hold of the walls bespeaks a feminine hand on the
hammer. There are several calendars, and there are quite an uncountable collection
of photograph frames, which fall over unless they are propped against something.
Most of the photographs are old and faded, and they are nearly all of babies. Babies
clothed and unclothed; babies with bare feet and little night-shirts on; babies suck-
ing their thumbs; babies lying prone on fur carriage-rugs; babies riding on their
mamma's backs, or sitting on their mamma's knees; babies crowing or crying. No
one who has a baby ever fails to send this maiden lady a photograph of it.

Miss Lydia settled me with some cushions in my chair, and shut the doorway
leading to her bedroom beyond, where I caught sight of a painted iron bedstead,
and a small indiarubber hot-water bottle hanging from one of its knobs. It is Miss
Lydia's most cherished possession, and she generally speaks of it reverently as 'the
comfort of my life.'

Poor Miss Lydia! Hers must, I think, be a lonely life, sacrificed patiently to
an invalid and almost inarticulate sister, and yet it is the very solitude of this little
chamber which is one of the few privileges to which she lays claim. It is to this little
room, with its humble furnishings, that all her troubles are taken, and it is here by
the window that she can sit with folded hands and think perhaps of something in
life which surely poor Lydia has missed. It is here she prays for those whose sins
weigh far more heavily upon her than they do upon themselves, and it is here that
she can pause and question with gentle faith the perplexities of life.

Miss Lydia tells my sister that she makes a thorough examination of her room
every night before she goes to bed, to see if there is a burglar concealed anywhere.
The movable property in the tiny house is probably not worth many pounds, as a
pawnbroker appraises things, and it would be a hardened thief that could deprive
the sisters of their small possessions; but the dread remains—the dread of burglars

and the dread of mice. Were it not for the look of the thing, she would almost rather discover a burglar than a mouse—'for at least burglars are human,' she explains, 'and one might be able to reason with them or pray for them, but who shall control the goings of a mouse?'

Sometimes these fears become quite a terror to Lydia Blind, and she once said that she felt so defenceless, that she thought it would be a great comfort to have a male defender to protect her.

It is the only unmaidenly remark she ever made, and it makes her blush in the dark when she thinks of it. She believes everyone remembers it with as vivid a distinctness as she does, and she trembles to think what sort of construction may have been put upon her words by ill-natured or thoughtless persons. It is a real trouble to her; but then all her troubles are real, and so are her bitter repentances over perfectly imaginary sins. But she has her little room and her faded photographs—life has its consolations.

CHAPTER IV

KATE JAMIESON, who is the independent member of The Family, and has been in a situation for some years as companion to a lady at Bath, has written home what she calls a 'joint letter' to apprise the whole of her family at one and the same time that she is engaged to be married. The excitement which this letter produced in the little household is hardly possible to describe. The news arrived when the Jamiesons were at breakfast. Perhaps I should mention, before going any further, that the Jamiesons' only extravagance is to take in three daily papers. One is an evening paper, which arrives at breakfast-time, and the other two are morning publications, which arrive at the same hour. It is customary for the members of this family each to read their own particular paper aloud during the entire meal, the rest of the party read their letters to each other, and there are still left several voices to demand what you will have for breakfast, to inquire how you have slept, and to comment upon the weather. So that from half-past eight until nine a cross-fire of conversation is going on all the time. . . .

'I see Hearne has scored sixty-eight at cricket, not out. That's not bad, you know. Kent ought to be looking up. The Australians are doing well. Yorkshire might do better. Extraordinary! Here's this chap who promised so well, bowled for a duck!' This from the eldest son of the House of Jamieson; while at precisely the same moment may be heard the voice of Maud: 'I must say I am rather astonished at the way boleros have remained in. This is one of the prettiest designs I have seen this year. How soon one gets accustomed to small sleeves. Well, I cannot say I like these Chesterfield fronts.'

Mrs. Jamieson is meanwhile reading aloud the columns of births, deaths, and marriages from beginning to end. Her limited acquaintance with the outside world might seem to preclude her from any vivid interest in those who must necessarily only be names to her, yet she finds subject-matter for comment through the entire perusal of the column. Needless to say, Mrs. Jamieson inclines to regard only the sadder aspects of these natural occurrences, and her comments thereupon are full of a sort of resigned melancholy. From her corner of the table may be heard the plaintive words: 'Here's a young fellow of twenty-four taken,' or, 'Fourscore years, well, well, and then passed away!' While the happier news of birth provokes her to hark back to an announcement of a similar nature in the family, perhaps only a year ago, and to talk of the responsibilities and the expense that the poor young couple will have to undergo. Mettie, who spends the greater part of every day writing letters, and whose chief joy in life is to receive them, reads the whole of her correspondence aloud from beginning to end, while Margaret Jamieson, behind the teapot, is letting off rapid volleys of questions respecting individual tastes about cream and sugar, and the Pirate Boy offers ham-and-eggs or sausages in a deep stentorian bass.

In the midst of this confusion of noise, when only a Jamieson, whose ear is curiously trained to it, can possibly hear what is being said, Mrs. Jamieson bursts into tears and, in the strong Kentish dialect of her youth, exclaims: 'Here's our Kate going to be married!' After the first burst of delighted surprise, there is a family feeling of apology towards Maud. That Kate should marry first is surely a little disloyal to the beauty of Belmont, and Mrs. Jamieson goes so far as to say: 'Never mind, Maud, it will be your turn next.'

After that, they all, singly and severally, recall their previously-expressed opinion that they knew something was up, and that certainly Kate could not have given them a more pleasant or more unexpected surprise.

The letter is then read aloud, and it is so long that one is glad to think that the absent Kate did not attempt to duplicate it, but contented herself with the Pauline method of one general epistle. With the Jamieson characteristic of telling everything exhaustively, Kate writes:

'Mr. Ward is not at all bad-looking; a little hesitating in his manner, and inclined to be untidy—you see, I am telling you everything quite candidly—but of course I can remedy all these defects when we are married. He has a short brown moustache, and rather a conical-shaped head.' (This is a fault that one feels Kate will not be able to remedy, even when she has married him.) 'He looks clever, though I do not think he is, very; he is well-connected, but does not know all his best relations. Poor, but with generous instincts'—one feels as though a cheiromancist were reading a client's palm—'well-read, but without power of conveying intelligence to others; hair rather thin and (I am afraid), false teeth; very religious, but I consider this in him more temperament than anything else. He has had a hard life, and not always enough to eat, until his uncle died, but now he could be quite independent if he liked, but he prefers the position which a Government appointment gives him.

'I hope to bring him down to stay when I return; please let him have the south bedroom, as that is the warmest, and I do not think James is very strong. I should like him to have a fire at night—I can arrange that with mother, as I feel quite well off now. We are to be married in July, and I am giving up my post here at once, so as to see something of you all before I go away.'

At this point the letter referred once more to Mr. Ward's personal appearance, and the description was of so great length that when Margaret Jamieson, who had run all the way from her home to ours to give it to us to read, asked me breathlessly what I thought about it, I determined to leave unread the remaining paragraphs, and to judge for myself of the bridegroom when he should come to Belmont and we should be invited to meet him.

'There is one thing,' said Mrs. Jamieson, when at the request of The Family, Palestrina went to sit with her one afternoon a few weeks later, to support her through the trying ordeal of waiting for Kate and 'James,' as he is now familiarly called, to arrive; 'the girls have nothing to be ashamed of in their home.' She looked with a certain amount of pardonable pride at the clean white curtains, and we gathered that we were meant to comment upon their early appearance. The white curtains,

Palestrina says, are not usually put up at Belmont until the first week in May.

'They look very handsome,' I said. It was a Jamieson afternoon—very wet, but clearing up about sundown, and Palestrina had suggested my escorting her as far as Belmont. But the rain came down in torrents again, when I would have started to return home, and the good Jamiesons begged me to stay, to avoid the chance of a chill, and to meet James.

'It is the first break in the family,' said Mrs. Jamieson tearfully, 'since poor Robert died. But, as James says, he hopes I am gaining a son, and not losing a daughter.' From which I gathered that James was a gentleman given to uttering rather a stale form of platitude.

All were waiting in a state of great trepidation the arrival of the engaged couple, and it was quite hopeless to avoid the encounter, for the rain descended in sheets outside, and preparations for supper seemed to be going on in the dining-room at Belmont. It was decided, by universal consent, that only Mrs. Jamieson and Palestrina and I should be in the drawing-room at the moment when they should enter. The presence of strangers, it was thought, would make it easier for James at the meeting where all were kinsfolk except himself. With their usual consideration, The Family decided that the rest of their large number should afterwards drop in casually, two by two, and be introduced to the new brother-in-law without ceremony. Mrs. Jamieson, who had not left the house that day, nor for many days previously, having been absorbed in preparations for the expected guest, was dressed in a bonnet and her favourite jacket with the storm-collar, which, as she explained to my sister, took away from the roundness of her face and gave her confidence.

Her habitual shyness, added to her fears of the unknown in the shape of the future son-in-law, had wrought her into a sort of rigid state in which conversation seemed impossible, and although we did our best to divert her attention, I am doubtful if she heard a word we said.

'They should be here soon,' I remarked presently.

Mrs. Jamieson, following some line of thought of her own, remarked that the first marriage in a family was almost like a death; and to this mournful analogy I gave assent.

'Kate says he is quite a gentleman,' hazarded Mrs. Jamieson, still rigid, and now white with anxiety and shyness.

I found myself replying, without overdone brilliance, that that seemed a good thing.

The sands of Mrs. Jamieson's courage were running very low. 'I hope he is not one of your grandees,' she said apprehensively; 'I would not like to think of Kate not being up to him. But their father was a gentleman—the most perfect gentleman I ever knew, and I have always that to think of. Still, a gentlemanly man is all I want for any of my girls, with no difference between the two families.'

Sometimes in this way Mrs. Jamieson gives one an unexpected insight into the difficulties of her life, and one feels that even her admiration for her daughters may be tinged with a slight feeling of being their inferior. I have heard her say, making use of a French expression such as she hazards so courageously, that there is something of the ' *grawn dam* about Maud;' and perhaps the loyal admiration thus expressed, may have been mingled with another sensation, not so pleasurable to the farmer's daughter.

I endeavoured to follow the intricacies of her train of thought, but the station omnibus had stopped at the gate, and the moment of supreme excitement had arrived.

Kate entered first. This was probably the crowning moment of her life. She came in with a little air of assurance that already suggested the married woman, and having kissed her mother, she said, in a proprietary sort of way: 'This is Mr. Ward, mamma.'

Mr. Ward has a curious way of walking on his toes; he came into the room as though tip-toeing across some muddy crossing on a wet day, and shook hands with a degree of nervousness that made even Mrs. Jamieson appear bold. One can hardly be surprised at Kate having mentioned that he has a conical-shaped head, for it is of the most strange pear-shape, and the sparse hair hangs from a ridge behind like a fringe. He sat down and locked his knees firmly together, with his clasped hands tightly wedged between them, while Kate made inquiries about the rest of the family, and I plunged heavily into remarks about the weather, and the state of the roads. It was a great relief when two of the sisters entered, in their best silk blouses, even although they repeated exactly what I had said a moment before about the weather and the mud. Five minutes later, according to preconceived arrangement, two other sisters came in and were kissed by Kate, and introduced by her to James. We had unconsciously taken up our position in two straight lines facing James, and it is no exaggeration to say that by this time shyness was causing great beads of perspiration to stand out on poor James's pear-shaped head. 'Surely they will spare him any more introductions before supper,' I thought; but the door had again opened, and Mettie and the Pirate Boy entered, and some unhappy chance was causing these last comers to comment upon the weather and the state of the roads, and to extend the line of chairs now facing James. We began to make feverish little remarks to each other, as though we were all strangers, and Palestrina asked Eliza if she were fond of dancing. George Jamieson, the eldest brother, was the last to enter the room, and Kate said: 'George, I am sure James would like to unpack before supper;' and the unhappy James tip-toed out between the two lines of chairs, with his eyes fixed upon the carpet.

'Well?' said Kate. And as The Family was The Family of Jamieson, that of course was a signal for each member of it to say the kindest thing that could possibly be said for the new arrival. Margaret found that he had kind eyes. And Eliza said: 'Not intellectual, but a good man.' Eliza, it must be remarked in passing, is the intellectual sister, with a passion for accurate information, and for looking up facts in the 'Encyclopædia Britannica.' Maud found that even his shyness was in his favour, and disliked men who made themselves at home at once. Mettie remarked that marriage was a great risk. This is one of poor little Mettie's platitudes, which she makes with faithful regularity upon all occasions. The Pirate Boy preferred, perhaps, a more robust development, and throwing out his own chest, he beat it with a good deal of violence, and said he would like to put on the gloves with Mr. Ward. Mrs. Jamieson could be got to say nothing but 'Poor fellow, poor fellow!' at intervals. But Gracie, the youngest daughter, remarked that she was sure that they would all get to like him immensely in time.

Kate looked grateful, and spoke with her usual fine common sense. 'What I say is,' she remarked, 'that of course no one sees James's faults more clearly than I do, but then I don't see why any of us should expect perfection. We haven't much to offer: I am sure I have neither looks, nor money, nor anything. And, after all, it's nice to think of one of us getting married—and I was no bother about it,' said the independent Kate, 'I mean, The Family had not to help, or chaperon me, or ask James down to stay.'

The sisters assented to this in a very hearty, congratulatory sort of way, and then, as the rain had ceased, I took my leave, but Palestrina was persuaded to stay and have supper. Kennie offered, in a doughty fashion, to see me home. The boy's kindness of heart constitutes him my defender upon many occasions, and he always looks disappointed if I do not take his arm. I do not think that the peaceful country road in the waning twilight could be considered a dangerous one, even to a cripple like myself; but Kennie, armed with a large stick and wearing a curious felt hat turned up at one side, appeared a most truculent defender, and regarded with suspicion all the pedestrians whom we met. Did but a country cart pass us, Kennie made a movement to ward off the danger of a collision with his arm. There is something in my helpless condition which, quite unconsciously I believe, produces a very valorous frame of mind in the Pirate, and he beguiled the whole of the way home with stories of his own prowess, and the hair-breadth escapes which he had had.

'I only once,' he said, 'had to take a human life in self-defence. Curiously enough'—Kennie's voice deepened, and he spoke with the air of a man who will spare a weak fellow-mortal all he can in the telling of his tale, and he enunciated all his words with a measured calm which was very impressive—'curiously enough, it was on the Thames Embankment!' Kennie cleared his throat, and dropping the deep bass voice of reminiscence, he began the history in a high-pitched tone of narrative. 'I was walking home alone one night from the City, when a very strange low fellow accosted me, and asked me for some money. The man's destitute appearance appealed to me, and unfortunately I gave him threepence. I suppose the action was about as dangerous a thing as I could have done. It showed that I had money, and I was practically defenceless while feeling in my pockets. The Embankment at that time of the evening was almost deserted; I could see the shipping in the river and the lights, and even passing cabs, but I was strangely alone, and still the man followed me. At last, in desperation, I raised my stick to drive him from me, and the next moment he had grappled with me! Instantly my blood was up!' The Pirate Boy stood still in the middle of the high-road, and went through a series of very forcible pantomimic gestures, and with awful facial contortions, indicative of violent exertions, he raised some imaginary object above his head and flung it from him. 'The next moment,' said Kennie,' I heard a splash. I had vanquished the man, and flung him far from me, straight from the Thames Embankment into the river.'

I was prepared to make an exclamation, but was prevented by Kennie, who said, in a dramatic sort of way, 'Wait!' and went on with his story. 'My instinct was to plunge after him, but I heard no sound, no cry, and from that day to this that struggle by the water's edge remains as one of the most vivid experiences of my life—in England, at least. But the man's end remains a mystery: I can tell you nothing more of him.'

'I think I would have fished the poor wretch out,' I said, and moved onwards on our walk, our pause in the public highway having lasted a considerable time,

'One learns rough justice out there,' said Kennie.

CHAPTER V

Miss TAYLOR was really responsible for the formation of the Stowel Reading Society, but Eliza Jamieson was her stanch supporter. Eliza drew the line at poetry and metaphysics, 'Neither of which,' she said, 'I consider an exact science.'

Miss Taylor said: 'But it is not a scientific course that I propose; it is English Literature in its fullest sense. I do think that Stowel is getting behind the rest of the world in its knowledge of the best literature, and I am sure that if a Reading Society were founded, The Uncle would be pleased to choose books and send them to us from London.'

To no one, perhaps, is the specializing definite article felt to be more appropriate than to Sir John. It seems to distinguish him from ordinary human beings; and it is felt to be indicative of a considerable amount of good taste and good feeling on the part of the Taylors, to drop the General's title when conversing with their intimate friends, and to refer to him merely as 'The Uncle.' When we call upon the Taylors we always ask how The Uncle is.

Eliza Jamieson became the society's secretary and. treasurer in one, and she it was who in her neat hand transcribed the letter, which all had helped to compose, to ask The Uncle what works in English literature it would be advisable for the Reading Society to get. His reply was read aloud at one of the first meetings, and each eulogised it in turn as being 'courtly,' 'gentlemanly,' 'manly,' and 'concise.' It could not but be felt, however, that as a guide to a choice of literature the letter was disappointing:

'DREA MADAM' (it ran),

'I much regret that I am unable to help you in any way about your books. I read very little myself, except the newspapers, though I occasionally take a dip into one of my old favourites by Charles Lever. I think a cookery-book is the most useful reading for a young lady, and she would be best employed studying that, and not filling her head with nonsense. This is the advice of a very old fellow, who remembers many charming girls years ago, who knew nothing about advanced culture. . . .'

It was a distinct salve to the Society's feelings to note that the letter was written on paper stamped with the address of a military club, and instead of copying it, and making an entry of it in the minutes of the Reading Society, it was pasted into the notebook, as it was thought the autograph and the crest were 'interesting.'

Since the foundation of the Reading Society, there has followed a period during which the young ladies of Stowel have written essays, and have met in each other's drawing-rooms to read poetry aloud, to their own individual satisfaction and to the torture of other ears.

Mrs. Fielden did not join the society, her plea being that poetry is merely prose with the stops in the wrong places, and therefore very fatiguing to read, and very obscure in its meaning. But Eliza has worn us out with books of reference, and we have become so learned and so full of culture, that it is impossible to say where it will all end. My own library has been ransacked for books—I think it is the fact of my having a library that has made our house a sort of centre for the Reading Society, We criticise freely all contemporary literature, and base our preference for any book upon its 'vigorous Saxon style.'

Eliza has written two reviews for the local newspaper, pointing out some mistakes in grammar in one of the greatest novels of the day, and this naturally makes us feel very proud of Eliza. Those of us who plead for an easy flowing style, consider that she has an almost hypersensitive ear for errors in the use of the English accidence. A split infinitive has, heretofore, hardly arrested our attention; now we shudder at its use, while the misuse of the word to 'aggravate,' which up to the present we believed in all simplicity to mean to 'annoy,' causes the gravest offence when employed in the wrong sense. Books from the circulating library have been known to be treated almost like proof-sheets, and corrections are jotted down in pencil on the margin of the leaves. Even the notes which ladies send to each other are subject to revision at the hands of the recipient. Ordinary conversation is now hardly known in Stowel, and tea-parties take the form of discussions. The spring weather is so warm that I generally have my long chair taken on to the lawn in the afternoons, and tea is sometimes brought out there when the meetings of the Reading Society are over. But tea, and even pound-cake, are thrown away upon young ladies who partake of it absently, and to whom all things material and mundane—these words are often used—must now be offered with a feeling of apology.

Major Jacobs rode over to see me this afternoon, and we had not long enjoyed the repose of long chairs and cigarettes under the medlar-tree, and the songs of birds which have begun nesting very early this year, and the quiet rumbling of heavy waggons that pass sometimes in the high-road beyond the garden, when the Reading Society in a body joined us from the house, and I heard my sister give directions for tea to be brought out on to the lawn. The other day I heard Palestrina tell a friend of hers that she nearly always contrived to have someone to tea, or to sit with Hugo in the afternoon, and my sister's satisfaction increases in direct proportion to the number of people who come.

We had hardly finished tea, before Frances Taylor said suddenly, yet with the manner of one who has risen to make a speech on a platform: 'Was Coleridge a genius or a crank?'

Eliza, assuming the deep frown of learning which is quite common amongst us nowadays, was upon her in a moment, and said emphatically: 'How would you define a genius?' The Socratic habit of asking for a definition is one that is always adopted during our discussions, and it is generally demanded in the tone of voice in which one says 'check' when playing chess. Frances Taylor was quite ready for Eliza, and said: 'Genius, I think, is like some star—'

'—Analogy is not argument!' Eliza pounced upon her in the voice that said, 'I take your pawn.'

It will be noticed, I fear, that in Stowel we are not altogether original in our arguments—many of them can be traced, alas! to the 'Encyclopaedia Britannica,' and they are not often the outcome of original thought.

Frances Taylor's king was once more in check, and she became a little nervous and irritable. 'I do not think we need go into definitions,' she said; but Eliza had gone indoors to 'look it up.' She returned presently with a dictionary, walking across the lawn towards us with it held close to her nearsighted eyes. 'A genius,' she began, and then she glanced disparagingly at the title of the book, and said, 'according to Webster, that is—but I do not know if we ought to accept him as a final authority— is explained as being "a peculiar structure of mind which is given by Nature to an individual which qualifies him for a particular employment; a strength of mind, uncommon powers of intellect, particularly the power of invention." A crank,' she went on, 'in its modern meaning, seems hardly to have been known to the writer of this dictionary; the word is rendered literally, as meaning "a bend or turn." '

'Then I submit,' said Miss Taylor, 'that Coleridge was a genius.'

Miss Tracey said in a very sprightly manner—she often astonished us by showing a subtle turn of mind, and a graceful aptitude for epigram which, it was believed, would only find its proper field in those salons which are now, alas! things of the past: 'Let us write him down a genius *and* a crank! The two'—she advanced her daring view bravely—'the two are often allied.' She had a volume of Coleridge on her bookshelves, and prided herself upon her appreciation—unusual in a woman— of the 'Ancient Mariner.'

'A genius in s, and a crank followed by a mark of interrogation!' said Eliza in a brilliant fashion, and Miss Taylor, not to be beaten in a matter of intellect, said at once: 'Did Bacon write Shakespeare's plays?'

Mrs. Gallup and Mr. Lee were quoted extensively.

Miss Taylor could only suggest, with a good deal of quiet dignity, that she could write to The Uncle and find out who is right. This of course closes the controversy for the present.

George Jamieson, who goes to town every day, gains advanced views from the magazines which he reads during his dinner-hour in the City, and he is a great assistance to the Reading Society. I contribute the use of my library, and I have heard the members of the Reading Society say that 'women are the true leaders of the present movement, and already their influence is being felt by the male mind.'

George brought with him the current number of the *Nineteenth Century* when he came home last Friday, instead of *Pearson'* s or the *Strand,* and already there are whispers of a Magazine Club in Stowel. Miss Frances Taylor received nothing but books on her last birthday, and Palestrina told me a pathetic little story of how Gracie Jamieson went without a pair of shoes to buy a copy of Browning. Perhaps the climax of culture and learning was felt only to have been reached when Eliza introduced the expression 'Hypothesis of Purpose' into an ordinary conversation at the conclusion of one of the meetings of the Reading Society.

After this, as Palestrina remarked, it was quite refreshing to hear that the curate's wife had got a new baby. It was born on Sunday, and the anxious father spent his days bicycling wildly to and fro between his own house and the church, hopelessly confusing his reading of the service, and then flying back to inquire about his wife's health. Led by him, we prayed successively for fine weather and for rain, while the Sunday-school teachers' meeting was announced for 2 a.m. on the following Saturday, and the Coal Club notices were inextricably confused with the publishing of banns of marriage. After each service the distracted little man would leap on his bicycle again, and scattering the departing congregation with his bicycle bell, he was off down the hill to his house. His perturbation was nothing compared with the confusion at home where, so far as I could make out, the bewildered household did nothing but run up and down stairs, and madly offer each other cups of tea.

My sister's kind heart suggested that we should have Peggy, the eldest child, to stay with us till her mother should be better. Is it necessary to mention the fact that Palestrina is fat and very pretty, and that she spoils me dreadfully? Do I want a book, I generally find that Palestrina has written for it, almost before I had realized that life was a wilderness without it. I have never known her out of temper, nor anything else but placid and serene. And she has a low, gurgling laugh, and a certain way of saying: 'Oh, that will be very nice!' to any proposal that one makes, which one must admit makes her a very charming, and a very easy person to live with. She is fond of children, and she announced to Peggy, with a beaming smile this morning, that she had a new little brother.

Peggy went on quietly with her breakfast for some time without making any remark; then she gave a little sigh, and said: 'Mamma thought she had enough children already, but I suppose God thought otherwise.'

Peggy has been in low spirits all day, and closely following some line of reasoning of her own, she has flatly refused to say her prayers at bed-time.

Mrs. Fielden rode over to see us this morning, in her dark habit, and neat boots which she loves to tap with her riding-crop. She came into the dim hall like the embodiment of Spring or of Life, and sat down in her oddly-shaped habit, as though she were at home, and was in no hurry to go off anywhere else. This gives a feeling of repose to a sick man. One knew that she would probably stop to luncheon, and that one would not have to say to her half a dozen times in the morning, 'Please don't go.'

Presently Margaret Jamieson, who had been doing the whole work of the curate's household during the late trying time, came with the baby in her arms to show him to Palestrina. Her manner had a charming air of matronliness about it, and she threw back the fretted silk of the veil that covered the face of the little creature in her arms, with an air of pride that was rather pretty to see. But Eliza, who had raced over to our house in the Jamieson usual headlong fashion, to say something to us on the subject of textual criticism, looked severely at the infant through her glasses, and remarked that she had no sympathy whatever with that sort of thing. Margaret hugged the baby closer to her, and Mettie, who had pattered over to see us with her cousin Eliza, remarked that children and their upbringing were doubtless among the great risks of matrimony.

'I am sure,' said Eliza, 'when one sees how happy Kate is with James, it makes one feel that marriage is not so very great a risk after all.'

That there should be an element of sarcasm in this remark did not even suggest itself to Eliza.

'We should all be thankful,' piped forth Mettie, who is always ready to talk, 'that it has turned out so well. Kate's courage and independence of mind seem exactly suited to Mr. Ward. But that is what I think about us all at Belmont; our characteristics are so different, that any gentleman coming amongst us might find something to attract him in one, if not in the others. Margaret is our home-bird, and Eliza is so cultured, and Kate—'

The two Miss Jamiesons were looking very uncomfortable, and Margaret said: 'Oh, Mettie, dear!' while Mrs. Fielden made an excuse for walking over to the piano. There was a piece of music open upon it. 'Do sing it,' she said to Palestrina.

THE GAY TOM-TIT.

A tom-tit lived in a tip-top tree, And a mad little, bad little bird was he. He'd bachelor tastes, but then—oh dear! He'd a gay little way with the girls, I fear! Now, a Jenny wren lived on a branch below, And it's plain she was vain as ladies go, For she pinched her waist and she rouged a bit, With a sigh for the eye of that gay tom-tit. She sighed, 'Oh my!' She sighed, 'Ah me !' While the tom-tit sat on his tip-top tree-tree-tree. And she piped her eye A bit-bit-bit For the love of that gay tom-tit-tit-tit.

She saw that her rouge did not attract, So she tried to decide how next to act: She donned a stiff collar and fancy shirt, And she wore, what is more, a divided skirt. Then she bought cigarettes and a big latch-key, And she said,' He'll be bound to notice me!' But she found her plan did not work one bit, For he sneered, as I feared, did that gay tom-tit. He sneered, 'Oh my!' He sneered, 'Oh lor! What on earth has she done that for-for-for?' And he winked his eye A bit-bit-bit, That giddy and gay tom-tit-tit-tit.

'Alas! no more,' said the poor young wren, Will I ape the shape of heartless men!' So she flung cigarettes and big latch-key With a flop from the top of the great green tree. And she wouldn't use rouge or pinch her waist, But she dressed to the best of a simple taste; Then she learned to cook and sew and knit— 'What a pearl of a girl!' said the gay tom-tit. Said he, 'Good day!' Said she, 'How do?' They were very soon friends, these two-two-two. And I'm bound to say In a bit-bit-bit, She married that gay tom-tit-tit-tit.

Thus sang Palestrina.

'Ethically considered, my dear Palestrina,' said Eliza, 'that song is distinctly unmoral.'

'Don't let us consider it ethically,' said Palestrina tranquilly; and she went over and sat in the corner of the sofa with several pillows at her back.

'Ethically considered,' repeated Eliza, 'that song, if one pursues its teaching to a logical conclusion, can only mean that all female social development is impossible, and that the whole reason for a woman's existence is that she may gratify man.'

They are really not worth it,' murmured Mrs. Fielden, who was in a frivolous mood.

'And mark you,' said Eliza, in quite the best of the Reading Society manner: 'it does not suggest that that gratification may be inspired either by our beauty, or by our intellect; indeed, it proves that such powers are worthless to inspire it. It postulates the hypothesis'—Eliza is really splendid—'that man is a brute whose appreciation can only be secured by ministering to his desire for food and suitable clothing, and that woman's whole business is to render this creature complacent.'

'Don't you think things are much pleasanter when people are complacent?' said my sister easily.

Eliza fixed her with strong, dark eyes. 'Were I describing you in a book,' she said—one feels as though Eliza will write a book, probably a clever one, some day— 'I should describe you as a typical woman, and therefore a pudding. A dear, tepid pudding, with a pink sauce over it. Very sweet, no doubt, but squashy—decidedly squashy. Some day,' said Eliza triumphantly, 'you will be squashed into mere pulp, and you will not like that.'

This did not seem to be a likely end to Palestrina. Eliza continued: 'Who will deny that men are selfish?'

'But they are also useful,' said Mrs. Fielden, in an ingenuous way. 'They open doors for one, don't you know, and give one the front row when there is anything to be seen, even when one wears a big hat; and they see one into one's carriage—oh! and lots of other useful little things of that sort.'

'Admitted,' said Eliza, 'that women have certain privileges—have they any Rights?'

Mrs. Fielden admitted that they had not. 'But,' she said, 'I don't really think that that is important. The men whom one knows are always nice to one, and I don't think it matters much what the others are.'

'Rank individualism,' said Eliza. And she said it without a moment's hesitation, which gave us a very high opinion indeed of her powers of speech. 'It is the fashion to say that each woman has only one man to manage, and she must be a very stupid woman if she cannot manage him; but there are thousands of women who, being weaker morally and physically than their particular man, can do nothing with him, and it is not fair to leave her wrongs unredressed, so long as you are comfortable and happy.'

'Still, you know,' said Mrs. Fielden thoughtfully, 'one cannot help wishing that they could get what they want without involving us in the question. You see, if they got their rights we should probably get ours too, and then I'm afraid we should lose our privileges.'

'You are like the man,' said I, 'who could do quite well without the necessaries of life, but he could not do without its luxuries.'

'What a nice man it must have been who said that!' exclaimed Mrs. Fielden. 'It would be quite easy to do without meat on one's table, but it would be impossible to dine without flowers and dessert.'

It must be admitted that Eliza had the last word in the argument after all.

'Just so,' she said; 'and all life shows just this—that a woman has, with her usual perverseness, chosen a diet of flowers and dessert with intervals of starvation, instead of wholesome meat and pudding.'

CHAPTER VI

'WE shall have to ask the engaged couple to dinner, I said to Palestrina one morning a few days later. 'And I suppose one or two more of the rest of The Family would like to be asked at the same time.'

'I never know in what quantities one ought to ask the Jamiesons,' said my sister, 'nor how to make a proper selection. It seems invidious to suggest that Kate and Eliza and Margaret should come, and not Maud and Gracie; and yet, what is one to do? The last time that you were away from home I wrote and said, "Will a few of you come?" And Mrs. Jamieson, the Pirate Boy, and four sisters came.'

'One feels sure,' I replied, 'that the Jamiesons thought that was quite a modest number to take advantage of your invitation. One knows that had they been inviting some girls from a boarding-school, they would have included the entire number of pupils.'

Palestrina protested that as the meal to which our friends were to come was dinner, it would be only reasonable to invite the same number of ladies and gentlemen; and to this I assented. She suggested asking the Darcey-Jacobs, whom we had not seen for a long time.

Mrs. Darcey-Jacobs is a woman who always affords one considerable inward amusement, being herself, I believe, more conspicuously devoid of humour than any one else I have ever met. Mrs. Darcey-Jacobs has never been known to see a joke. That she herself should appear to anyone in a humorous light, would, I know, appear an inconceivable contingency to her. She has a high Roman nose, and rather faded yellow hair, which was her principal claim to beauty when a girl. It is even now thick and long, and is always worn in a sort of majestic coronet on the top of her head. Her manner is somewhat formidable and emphatic, and the alarm which this engenders in timid or diffident persons is increased by the habit she has of accentuating many of her remarks by a playful, but really somewhat severe rap over the knuckles of the person she is addressing, with her fan or lorgnettes. She dresses handsomely in expensive materials somewhat gaudy in colour, and she has an erect carriage, of which she is very proud. Mrs. Darcey-Jacobs has a good deal to say on the subject of the feeblemindedness of the male sex, and when something has been proved impossible of attainment by them, she always says, 'A woman could have done it in five minutes.'

At the time of her marriage, Mrs. Darcey-Jacobs (Miss Foljambe, she was then) was a dowerless girl with two admirers, Major Jacobs and Mr. Morgan. Not being, it would seem, a young lady of very deep affections, her choice of a husband was decided entirely by the extent of the worldly prospects he could offer, and the Major being the better match of the two, was accepted. But how cruel are the tricks that fate will sometimes play! Not long after her marriage, Mr. Morgan not only inherited a large fortune, but shortly afterwards left this world for a better, and Mrs. Darcey-Jacobs is in the habit of remarking, with a good deal of feeling, 'If I had only chosen the other I might have been a happy widow now!'

Mrs. Darcey-Jacobs lives in our quiet country neighbourhood during the greater part of the year, on the distinct understanding that she loathes every hour of it. When she goes abroad or to London, she talks quite cheerfully of having had one breath of life. So fraught with happy successes are these pilgrimages in her brocaded satin gowns into the outer world, that she often says that were she but free, she might have the world at her feet to-morrow. And she has been known to refer to the Major, still in the tone of cheerful resignation and with her emphasizing tap of the fan, as 'a dead weight round her neck.'

The Major himself is a guileless person, whose very simplicity causes his wife more exquisite suffering than even a husband of keen vindictive temper could inflict.

Does Mrs. Jacobs give a dinner-party, it is not unusual for the master of the house to remark in a congratulatory tone from his end of the table, 'What has Mullens been doing to the silver, my dear; it looks unusually bright?' While his greeting to his friends as they arrive at his house, though distinctly cordial, often takes the form of a hearty 'I had no idea that we were going to see you to-night.' As Mrs. Darcey-Jacobs always sends some kind message from the Major in her notes of invitation, this of course is most disconcerting, both for her and for her guests. This year when they were in Italy, a friend of ours in the same hotel overheard a lady ask the Major if he were related to the Darceys of Mugthorpe. 'I really can't tell you,' said the Major; 'the Darcey was my wife's idea.'

'Four Jamiesons,' I said, 'and the Darcey-Jacobs, and our two selves. Isn't it humiliating to think that we have invariably to invite the same two men to balance our numbers at a dinner-party? I can't help remarking that Anthony Crawshay and Ellicomb are present at every dinner-party in this neighbourhood, as surely as soup is on the table.'

'We might ask Mrs. Fielden,' said Palestrina; she is sure to have some Colonels with her. Besides, I love Mrs. Fielden, though people say she is a flirt. I think most men are in love with her; some propose to her, and some do not, but they all love her.'

'Even when she refuses to marry them?'

'I have heard Mrs. Fielden say that an offer of marriage should be refused artistically,' said Palestrina. 'She says young girls hardly ever do it properly, and that they are brusque and brutal. I suppose she herself has some charming way of her own of refusing men which does not hurt their feelings. I believe,' said Palestrina, 'that she would marry Sir Anthony Crawshay if he could play Bridge.'

'Anthony is an excellent fellow,' I said.

Mr. Ellicomb is a young man of High Church principles and artistic tastes, who has taken an old Tudor farmhouse in the neighbourhood, and has furnished it very well. He waxes eloquent on the monstrous inelegance of modern dress, and the decadence of Japanese art, and he says he would rather sit in the dark than burn gas in his house, and he dusts his own blue china himself. In his house it is a sign of art to divert anything from its proper use, and to use it for another purpose than that for which it was originally intended. Poor Ellicomb uses a cabbage-strainer as a fern pot, a drain-tile for an umbrella-stand, his mother's old lace veils as antimacassars, bed-posts as palm-stands, a linen press as a book-case, and a brass spittoon for growing lilies. It is almost like playing at guessing riddles to go over his house with him, and to try and discover for what purpose some of his things were originally created. Their conversion to some other use is, I am sure, a very high form of art.

'There are the Jamiesons,' said my sister, as we sat in the hall ready to receive our guests.

It does not require any occult power to sit indoors and to be able to distinguish the Jamiesons' carriage-wheels from those of the other arrivals, for the Jamiesons have, as usual, employed the 'six-fifty' bus on its return journey from the station to set them down at our gate. It is quite a subject of interest with our neighbours to find themselves fellow-passengers with the young ladies, in their black skirts and their more dressy style of bodice concealed beneath tweed capes. And it generally gets about in Stowel circles before the evening is over, or certainly soon after the morning shopping has begun, that the Miss Jamiesons have been dining at such or such a house. Even the bus conductor has a sympathetic way of handing the young ladies into his conveyance when they are going out to dinner, and he fetches a wisp of straw and wipes down the step if the night is wet.

Mr. Ward piloted the independent Kate up the short carriage-drive with quite an affectionate air of solicitude, frequently inquiring of her if she did not feel her feet a little damp; and Kate answered cheerfully and kindly, and felt, no doubt, that this sort of fussing was one of the drawbacks of prospective matrimony, but that it was only right to accept the little attentions in the spirit in which they were made. The Pirate Boy, who followed with his sister Maud, begged her to take his arm in a burly fashion, and fell a little distance behind. The Pirate Boy thinks that it is etiquette to place himself at a distance from any engaged couple, even during the shortest walk. He does so even when he makes the untoward third in a party. On these occasions he falls behind and puts on an air of abstraction, a little overdone. The Jacobs arrived next, and then Anthony Crawshay, who drove over in his high dog-cart, with its flashing lamps and glittering wheels—a very good light running cart it is; Anthony and I used often to drive in it together—and Ellicomb arrived in a brougham, in which we have a shrewd suspicion there is a foot-warmer.

Maud began to flirt with Mr. Ellicomb directly. I have never known her to be for long in the society of a gentleman without doing so, and her sisters are wont to say of Maud that she certainly has her opportunities, while the criticism of an unprejudiced observer might be that she certainly makes them. Mr. Ellicomb, it is believed, has written an article in one of the magazines on the reformation of men's clothing, and it is hoped he will become a member of the Reading Society. He ate very little at dinner, and talked in a low, cultured voice about Church matters the whole of the evening, and uttered some very decided views upon the subject of the celibacy of the clergy.

'I must say,' said Major Jacobs, 'that I also approve of celibacy in the Church, and I may say in the army and in the navy. If I had my life to live over again—'

'William!' said Mrs. Darcey-Jacobs, in an awful voice.

William was about to retreat precipitately from his position, but catching sight perhaps of a sympathetic eye turned upon him from that good comrade of his, Anthony Crawshay, he blundered on:

'If Confession, now, became more general in the English Church,' he said, 'secrets confided to the clergy could hardly be kept inviolate. A clergyman's wife might almost—well, not to put too fine a point on it—wring from him by force the secret that had been committed to him.'

'I hope so, indeed,' said Mrs. Darcey-Jacobs.

'The Anglican Church,' said Mr. Ellicomb,' recognises that difficulty, and has met it in the persons of the Fathers of the Church.'

Maud Jamieson raised soft eyes to his, and said that a woman might be a help and a comfort to a man.

Mr. Ellicomb seemed disposed to admit that it might be so. 'I have been in retreat at Cowley for some weeks,' he said, 'and the cooking was certainly monstrous, and would you believe it, they did not allow one to bring one's own servant with one.' There is nothing monkish about Ellicomb himself, nor is his asceticism overdone.

'I have been reading a book on sects and heresies,' said Mrs. Fielden, 'and I find

I belong to them all.'

Mr. Ellicomb interposed eagerly by saying, 'If I had to state my own convictions exactly, I should certainly say that I was a Manichaean, with just a touch of Sabellianism.'

'I think,' said Mrs. Fielden gravely, 'that I am a Rosicrucian heretic'

Mr. Ellicomb was interested and delighted. 'I know,' he said, 'that many people would think that I had not exactly stated my position. For instance, a lady to whom I described my symptoms the other day, told me at once that I was a Buddhist by nature, and an Antinomian by education, and I felt that in part she was right.'

Mrs. Darcey-Jacobs here interposed, and gave it as her opinion emphatically, that man was a contemptible creature, whatever his beliefs might be, and that he required a woman to look after him. 'To look after him,' she repeated, in a tone that said as plainly as possible, 'to keep him in order,' and she tapped Mr. Ellicomb sharply on the knuckles.

The Pirate Boy had some brave notions about what he called The Sex, and here plunged into a long description of how he had rescued a fair creature out of the hands of cut-throats out there, and he illustrated his action of saving the fair one by holding an imaginary six-shooter to Palestrina's head in a very alarming way. He talked of man as The Protector, and thrust his hand into his cummerbund—the action I suppose, being intended to show that the six-shooter had been replaced—and glanced round the table with an air of defiance. 'There is not a man,' he remarked, 'I don't care who he is, if he fail in respect to a woman when I am present, that shall not get a decanter hurled straight at his head—straight at his head. I have said it!' He laid his hand impetuously upon one of two heavy cut-glass bottles that had been placed in front of me, and one trembled for the safety of one's guests. 'I remember,' he said, 'in one of those gambling-hells in the Far West, where there were about as unruly a set of fellows and cut-throats as ever I came across—' The rest of the story was so evidently culled from the last number of the *Strand Magazine* that it hardly seemed rude of Palestrina to interrupt it by bowing to Mrs. Fielden, and suggesting that they should adjourn. Maud Jamieson drew my sister aside as they stood grouped round the fireplace in the hall drinking their coffee, and thanked her for introducing Mr. Ellicomb to her. 'He is perfectly charming,' she said. But Maud's sisters have confided to us that this is her inevitable conclusion about the last man she has met, and it is intended as a sort of pre-vindication of herself. Maud, it seems, intends to flirt with everyone she meets, but if she pretends that her affections are really touched, there can be no upbraidings on the part of The Family.

Kate Jamieson sat on the sofa, and twisted her engagement ring complacently round her finger. She thought that Mr. Ward had carried himself very well this evening. His quietness throughout the dinner compared favourably with the conversation of other guests. Kate said once to Palestrina: 'He is a man that I shall feel the utmost confidence in taking about with me everywhere.' And the remark conveyed the suggestion that Mr. Ward would always be an appendage to Kate Jamieson.

Anthony Crawshay is a very good fellow indeed. The most advanced and cultured young lady will never get him to talk about metaphysics in the crush of a ball-room, nor to concern himself about the inartistic shape of the clothes we wear nowadays. 'If I didn't like them, I shouldn't wear them,' says Anthony. He is a short spare man, with a voice somewhat out of proportion to his size, and the best cross-country rider in the county. The habit he has got of shouting all his remarks, seems rather pleasantly in accordance with his honest nature. Anthony very seldom speaks of anyone of whom he has not a good word to say; but if he does mention anyone whom he dislikes, he does so in a very hearty manner, which is almost as good as many other people's praise. He is as obstinate, as straightforward, and as good a fellow as a country neighbour ought to be. 'We have been hunting a May fox, by Gad, Hugo,' said Anthony, and he began to tell me about the run—a thing I can hardly get anyone to do nowadays.

The Pirate Boy, upon whom the word 'horse' had a rousing effect, condemned the whole breed of English horses in one short speech. 'I assure you,' he said, getting up and sawing the air with his hand, 'there are some of those wild mustangs out there which would knock spots out of any horses in your stables.'

Thus challenged, Anthony, who was standing on the hearthrug, turned and, stooping towards me, asked, in what he intended to be a whisper, who the young fellow was, and shouted abroad: 'Rum chap that, very rum chap!'

By-and-by Maud Jamieson went to the piano and began to sing ballads to Mr. Ellicomb; and we have an inward conviction—Palestrina and I—that this evening's report to the Jamieson family will be that Mr. Ellicomb is 'struck.' Major Jacobs considers himself musical because he likes hearing the words of a song distinctly pronounced. He was charmed with Maud's singing, and Kate encouraged the girl in a little matronly way which she has lately assumed. She called forth Maud's best efforts by saying, 'What was the pretty Irish song you sang the other night Y or 'You haven't given us "We'd better bide a wee" yet, dear.' Maud responded with several ballads, and wished she had some of Lord Henry Somerset's songs with her, Mr. Ellicomb having expressed a fondness for them. An opportunity was thus given for suggesting a call at Belmont—Maud knows mamma will be delighted—she wished Kennie were more good at that sort of thing; the invitation to come in some afternoon might perhaps have come better from a brother.

It was very gratifying to find that Mr. Ward, fortified by dinner, became more courageous than I have ever known him to be before. He tip-toed almost boldly across the room, and sitting down beside my sister, began to make a series of deliberate remarks to her, mostly in the form of interrogation: 'Do you care for Scotch songs? 'Have you ever been in Ireland?' 'Do you know Wales at all?' And to these important questions Palestrina made suitable replies. 'That is *most* interesting,' I heard her say from time to time, using the formula of those who are bored to the extent of complete absence of mind.

Mrs. Fielden crossed the room suddenly, with a shimmer of silken skirts. In spite of her frivolity, she has a way of making herself necessary to every party to which she goes. There used to be an old saying long ago in Scotland that wherever The Macgregor sat was the head of the table. Mrs. Fielden is always the centre of every party, although she has a childish habit, which in another woman might be ascribed to shyness, of taking the least conspicuous sea\ in the room. Consequently, when she dispersed the little group that was standing or sitting about her, applauding everything she said, and came across the room in pink satin and roses and diamonds, and sat down beside my sofa, the action had something regal about it, as though she had left a throne and come to speak to me.

'I am going to teach you to play Bridge,' she said.

'That is most kind of you.'

'I am going to carry you off to Stanby next week to give you lessons,' she went on.

I have a strong conviction that if Mrs. Fielden were to give a beggar a halfpenny, he would probably stoop down and kiss the edge of her skirt, or do something equally unconventional and self-abasing. She might, as a great favour, give a court-ier who had risked his life for her, her hand to kiss. When she smiles, men become foolish about her.

'It is very kind of you to want us,' I said.

'I want Bridge,' said Mrs. Fielden, and, as usual when she is going to be provok-ing, she looked prettier than ever, and began to smile.

'Anyone will do to make up a rubber, I suppose?' I said.

'Oh yes, anyone,' said Mrs. Fielden.

'Consequently, my sister and I need not feel particularly distinguished by being asked,' I continued.

'I am so glad Palestrina is coming,' said Mrs. Fielden, 'because several men have written to tell me they are coming to stay, just when my sisters-in-law are leaving, and I suppose I oughtn't to entertain a houseful of men alone, ought I?'

Mrs. Fielden does exactly as she pleases upon all occasions, but this does not prevent her from pretending to have acute attacks of propriety sometimes.

'We will play Bridge and chaperon you with pleasure,' I said.

'I thought of drowning myself yesterday,' said Mrs. Fielden, 'because it rained all day, and I had no one to amuse me, and then I thought I would ask you to come over and play Bridge instead. When I am bored I never can make up my mind whether I shall commit suicide, or go into a convent, or get married. Which do you advise?'

'I should advise you to marry,' I said. 'So far as I can gather, a great source of discord and danger in our neighbourhood would be removed if you did so.'

Mrs. Fielden said with her eyes, 'Hugo, you are very cross.' But being the most good-natured woman in the world, and sharing that forbearance which most people extend to an invalid, she smiled instead.

'Why do you stay here when you are feeling so tired?' she said to me pres-ently.

'Because,' I replied, 'my sister lies awake half the night and thinks I am going to die, if I show any signs of fatigue, or go to bed early. Besides, for us, you know, this is quite an exciting evening. We have thought about our dinner-party for days past.'

'If you were nice,' said Mrs. Fielden after a pause,

'You would ask me to come into your library and smoke.'

'Do you smoke?'

'No,' said Mrs. Fielden, 'I don't.'

'I'm glad you don't,' I said.

'For years,' said Mrs. Fielden, 'I tried to think it was wrong, and then I quite enjoyed smoking, but there is a certain effort involved in trying to raise an innocent occupation to the level of a crime.'

'It is a very unfeminine habit,' I said; partly because I was in a contradictious mood, and partly because I wanted to snub Mrs. Fielden for being so beautiful and young and charming.

'The last man,' said Mrs. Fielden gravely, 'who made that remark, died shortly afterwards.'

She was gathering up my cushions and pillows as she spoke, and she turned to my sister as she crossed the hall, and said: 'We are going to study philosophy in the library.'

The library was lit by a single lamp, and the fire burned low in the grate; but the room was illumined suddenly by a pink dress and roses and diamonds, and Mrs. Fielden was arranging cushions, in the very skilful way she has, on my sofa by the fire. She handed me my cigarette-box and matches, and spread a rug over my leg. For some occult reason, the rustling pink dress only whispered softly over the carpet now, like a woman's hushed voice in a sick-room, and Mrs. Fielden, by the simple act of drawing up a chair to the fire and sitting in it, took the head of the table again, and became the centre of the room.

'May I really smoke,' I asked, 'after being such a brute as to say you mustn't?'

'I look upon smoking as a purely feminine habit, like drinking tea, or having headaches, or anything of that sort,' said Mrs. Fielden. 'It was simply because it was so expensive that men took to it in the first place. Ethics should not be based upon accident, should it?'

I handed Mrs. Fielden my cigarette-box.

'If you are quite sure you disapprove I will have one,' she said.

From the hall came the sound of Maud's singing. Her voice is not of great compass, nor very strong, but it is clear and fresh, with a tuneful cadence in it.

'You spend nearly all your days here?' said Mrs. Fielden, looking round the room.

'Until the afternoon,' I said; 'and then Palestrina and I go for a little walk, and at tea-time I go to the hall sofa, and she asks people to come up and sit with me.'

'I am glad you like books,' said Mrs. Fielden.

'But really,' I said, 'the good folks in Stowel are all extraordinarily kind to me, and some of the Jamiesons are up nearly every day.'

'I like the Jamiesons,' said Mrs. Fielden; 'they are so intelligent. Have you ever noticed that their watches all keep exact time, and that they tell you the hour to the very second. And they always know what day of the month it is, and when Easter falls, and how much stuff it takes to make a blouse.'

'You wrong Eliza Jamieson,' I said; 'she studies philosophy.'

'Oh,' said Mrs. Fielden eagerly, 'I forgot to tell you, I have begun to study philosophy. I began last week. Will you lend me some books, please? I want to be very wise and learned.'

'Why?' I asked.

'I think,' said Mrs. Fielden, 'that it might be nice if people did not always call one frivolous; and that if I studied philosophy—'

'I shall not lend you any books,' I said.

'That is rather disobliging of you.'

'Because,' I said, 'our lives should always show a perfect equation. If you are a frivolous person you should behave frivolously.'

'You mean as I am a frivolous person,' said Mrs. Fielden.

'As you are a frivolous person,' I repeated.

'And after all,' said Mrs. Fielden,' with a contemplative air, 'how silly philosophy is! I asked somebody the other day the meaning of a syllogism, and really I don't think I ever heard anything quite so foolish.'

'It is quite beneath your notice,' I said.

'I did think of asking you if I might come over sometimes and read these musty volumes of yours.'

'You would probably find them as uninteresting as I am,' I said.

Mrs. Fielden looked as if she thought that might be possible, and did not press the matter.

I dislike being disloyal to my books, for they are such good friends of mine. But a great wish came to me then, to get up and do something, instead of for ever reading the doings and the thoughts of other people. I thought how much I should like to live again, and just for once sleep on the veldt with the stars overhead, or that I could get astride of a horse, and follow a burst of the hounds over the wet fields in England. And so thinking, I turned on the sofa, and said petulantly, 'I wish Maud Jamieson would not sing that song.'

'Oh that we two were maying,' she sang, in the song that tells of love and separation, and the longings and heartbreaks which it is much better not to speak about, and the things which we want and cannot have.

'I hate yearners,' I said. 'Why can't she sing something cheerful?'

Mrs. Fielden rose from her chair by the fire and crossed the hearthrug, and came and sat down on my sofa. She took my hand in hers and said:' Poor boy! is it very hard sometimes?'

'Of course,' said Palestrina, as we went upstairs to bed after our guests had departed, 'you are sure to feel tired. The little party has been too much for you, I'm afraid. It was very tiresome for you, having to leave us all.'

'I felt rather a crock after dinner,' I said, 'and I think the hall gets hot in the evening.'

'I wish I could make you better,' said Palestrina affectionately; 'it is horrid for you being ill.'

'Everyone,' I said, 'makes far too much fuss about health. Why, ten officers of our regiment are buried in South Africa. I suppose half the pensioners in Chelsea Hospital have had wounds as bad as mine, and a cripple more or less in the world does not matter very much. Women are kind enough to pity me. They even confide their troubles to me sometimes, because I am a poor thing lying on a sofa. I am really quite happy hobbling about with you, Palestrina; and when I am older, I shall probably take an interest in the garden. There is a proper and philosophical attitude of mind in respect of these things.'

'Oh, Hugo,' said Palestrina, 'I always know you are not happy when you begin to be philosophical.'

'Life is very easily explained without the assistance of philosophy when everything goes all right,' I replied.

CHAPTER VII

HAVE I ever mentioned that Palestrina is engaged to be married? If I have not done so, it is because it seems an obvious fact that all Palestrinas are engaged. Her fiancé, who is called Thomas, is stationed with his regiment in Ireland. A few weeks ago he sent her, as a token of his affection, a yellow dog with long hair. Palestrina does not like dogs, but she is trying to love Down-Jock for Thomas's sake. She says his name is Jock. The dog is a curious creature, with a passion for hurling himself at those who wear clean flannel trousers or light skirts. Thomas says he is fall of intelligence. He appears to be quite a young animal, but he can affect the airs of extreme old age, sleeping in a basket a great part of the day, or standing on the door-step to bark at visitors in an asthmatical manner, as though he would say, 'I am too old and too feeble to give chase, but while I am alive this house shall not lack a defender.' At other times he is wildly juvenile, and rolls himself over and over in an exuberance of youthful fun. This is chiefly on Sundays, when (his best joke) he pretends he wants to come to church with us. Sunday is Down-Jock's happiest day in all the week. No Christian in the land loves it more than he does. He begins his religious exercises early in the morning by barking outside the doors of all those people who have determined to take an extra half-hour's rest, and he continues barking without ceasing until the sleeper awakes and gets out of bed to open the door for him. He bustles in and wags his tail cheerfully, saying as plainly as a dog can say it, 'I am an early riser, you see—and a teetotaler,' he adds, trotting across the room to the water-jug, and lapping full red tonguefuls of its contents. Then he stands in the middle of the room and barks at you; runs to the door and barks at it; barks at the servants as they go downstairs, promising—the little tell-tale!—that their lateness shall be reported in the proper quarter. Finally, he climbs on to the bed, and goes to sleep upon your feet.

During breakfast he is attentive to everyone, and sits on the skirts of those ladies who most dislike dogs, and pulls them down uncomfortably from the waist. He watches every mouthful of food that is eaten, and grudges it to the eater; and his eyes are saying all the time, 'How can you be so greedy?' After breakfast his most boisterous juvenile mood begins. He jumps on everyone, or rolls himself over and over under everyone's feet. He wags his tail, barks in a piercing manner—the bark of the gay young dog—and madly rushes after, imaginary rats. All gloves and shoes become his playthings, and he frolics blithely with the hat-brush.

On weekdays he pleads old age as an excuse, and refuses to come anywhere with us; but on the Sabbath morning, who so ready as Down-Jock to take his walks abroad? He flies after us to the gate, his long hair streaming in the wind, and his short legs racing like a clockwork dog.

Palestrina says: 'Oh dear, what shall we do? Down-Jock! down, sir! Oh, he has spoilt my dress! Good doggie, mustn't go to church! Go home! go home! Oh, Jock, do get down! Look, he is following us still, and the church door is always open; he is sure to come in in the middle of the service, and trot up to us in our pew. Do you think Thomas would mind if I were to look as if he didn't belong to us?'

Jock flies back with an old bone in his mouth and deposits it at Palestrina's feet, dares her to touch it, and makes flying snatches at her shoes when she kicks the treasure aside.

'I must take him back,' says Palestrina. 'It will make me late of course, but I must go and shut him up.'

'He won't follow you,' I say. 'He is quite determined to go to church.'

Palestrina lifts the heavy beast in her arms, and in an exuberance of joy Down-Jock makes a door-mat of her dress, and rubs his paw affectionately against it and licks her hand.

Of course he escapes presently and runs after us; that is his best and most killing joke. Inwardly one feels he is in a state of hardly suppressed laughter, as he tears down the road again, barking with glee. And then he gets a sober fit, walks demurely in front of us in the narrow field-path, changes his mind suddenly about going to church, stops dead short, and trips us up; thinks after all he ought to go to the morning service as an example to the servants; toddles on again, and stops to say (with the air of extreme old age again assumed) that, after all, he is not up to the exertion, and would have to sit down at the Psalms, so perhaps it really would be better to stay quietly at home. Another stop. A rapid toilet performed by scratching his head with his hind-leg, 'just in case I meet anyone coming out of church whom I know'; and then Down-Jock meets a boy friend strolling off to the fields, and, running up to him, says: 'One must conform to conventionalities, but between you and me, I never had the remotest intention of going to church.'

Down-Jock, in his moments of most restless activity, always reminds me of a servant of ours who has occasional fits of the most intense energy. It begins quite early in the morning, when she gets up some hours before her usual time, and gives a sort of surprise party to the rest of the household. These parties take place two or three times a year, and we do not get over them for weeks afterwards. Every room in the house is visited in turn, and delinquencies of a year are laid bare. During the morning, cupboards are turned out in a magisterial sort of way, and dusty corners are triumphantly displayed. The most cherished rubbish is freely consigned to the waste-paper baskets, and collections of all sorts are contemptuously swept away. We hastily gather up books and precious oddments, and hurry off with them to my den, where we take refuge till the whirlwind is past. Curtains and tablecloths are shaken, with a sort of vindictive energy, at the back-door; all windows are flung open, and rugs are rolled up, making a sort of obstacle race in every passage and room. Down-Jock, who never recognises a superior in anyone, is the only one of the party who is not rendered an abject coward. He unrolls rugs, and runs away with dusters, and snaps at the heels of the housemaid, in a way that provokes one's wonder at his temerity. My sister and I, having locked away our most cherished possessions, generally contrive to be out of the house as much as possible on one of these tempestuous days. And following the line of reasoning, not of the highest order, which suggests that if one cannot be happy, one had better try and be good, Palestrina always visits her old women at the workhouse on these days.

'I wish,' she said to me, 'that you would walk into the village and meet me on my way home. I don't think anybody is coming up to see you this afternoon, and the house is so uncomfortable when Janet is in one of her whirlwind moods. Come as far as the corner, and go in and sit down at old Pettifer's if you get tired.'

'Shadrach Pettifer tells me,' I said, 'that his affection for you is based on the fact that you are so like his poor old mother. Perhaps while I am waiting at his cottage he may give me further interesting facts about you.'

Shadey is an old man with a bent back and curious bright eyes that gleam under a heavy thatch of eyebrow. His wife is the very thinnest old woman that I have ever seen; her cheeks have fallen in and are so very wrinkled that they always remind me of a toy balloon that a child has pricked with a pin. She is always ill and never complaining. Any expression of sympathy seems foreign to her comprehension, and the 'Poor thing!' or 'I am so sorry,' so eagerly accepted by more fortunate folk, is received by her with a certain air of independence. Last winter Mrs. Pettifer was dangerously ill with internal gout, but expressions of condolence to her were always met with the rather curious reply, 'Well, you see, sir, we must have something to bring us to our end.' There is a whole world of philosophy in this.

To-day the old couple spent the time while I waited for Palestrina in their cottage, in describing to me the last days in the life of their tortoise, an old friend, and an animal of evidently strange and unusual qualities. Towards the close of its life it was, on the testimony of the Pettifers, taken with screaming fits, and it even had to be held down 'when the high-strikes was wuss.' Later, it used to run round and round as never was. And at last Shadey determined to release it from this earthly tabernacle. He asked his friend Bridgeman, Anthony Crawshay's head-keeper, to come round some evening and administer poison to the unfortunate beast, and the effect of the dose was as strange as it was unexpected. The poison was the first thing for weeks that poor Toots the tortoise had seemed to enjoy. It seemed, to quote again from the testimony of those most intimately acquainted with the animal, to 'put new life into Toots,' and the more poison that was administered, the livelier did he become, ' until he was that gay it seemed as if he would ha' laughed at yer!' Finally, I understood that when poison sufficient to kill two carthorses had been given, the afflicted animal yielded to treatment, and its shell now adorns the kitchen dresser.

We returned home to find the house smelling of furniture polish, and permeated with a certain cold primness which succeeds a tidying up, and can only be dispelled by a glowing fire. One by one, things were brought back to the hall, and we felt like snails creeping out in the evening after a day of rain. Banished property strewed the tables again, and Palestrina opened the piano and spread it with music. It was an act of defiance, but comfortable nevertheless, to collect the cushions which had been dotted primly about in clean muslin covers, and to pile them all on to the sofa before the fire. But Down-Jock, who always goes one better than anyone else, contributed still more completely to the systematized disorganization of the house. He gaily wiped his muddy feet on clean paint, tore blithely round after imaginary rats wherever order reigned. Finally, in an exuberance of joy, he made a hearty supper off Palestrina's manuscript book of music, and barked with glee.

And yet some people say that dogs are not intelligent!

CHAPTER VIII

THE UNCLE, Sir John, is coming to stay at the Taylors', and the town is in something of a flutter over this event. It was hoped that the Taylors would give a tea-party in honour of their guest, but there is a shrewd notion abroad that no one will be allowed to see very much of him, except at a distance. The Taylors had hoped that there would be some occasion during his visit, at which The Uncle might speak in public, and Mr. Taylor has tried, half jestingly, to induce his brother townsfolk to arrange what he calls 'something in the political line,' while the august relative is staying with him. I think we owe it to the fact that the political meeting was found to be an impossibility, that we were asked to tea at the Taylors'.

Invitations, instead of taking the form of a friendly note, after the pattern of Stowel invitations in general, were conveyed on one of Mrs. Taylor's visiting cards, with 'At home, Thursday the 17th, four to seven,' upon it. 'A little abrupt,' ladies of Stowel were inclined to think, but of course the Taylors are people of some importance in the place. No one quite knew how to answer the invitation, and a good many friendly little visits were paid on the afternoon on which they arrived, and the mysterious card was produced from a bag or purse, with the smiling apology, 'I am sure fashions change so quickly that one hardly knows how to keep up with them.' And then ideas were exchanged as to the reply suitable to such a form of invitation. Miss Tracey said that she always thought that an invitation was accepted in as nearly as possible the same manner in which it was given, and she announced that she and her sister meant to return one of their own visiting-cards to Mrs. Taylor, with the day and the hour named upon it, and 'With pleasure' written underneath. This was considered suitable, for the most part, but those who still had doubts upon the subject, made elaborate efforts to meet Mrs. Taylor during the morning's shopping, and to say to her, in a friendly way, 'We are coming, of course, on Thursday. Will you excuse our writing a note, at this busy time?'

The Miss Blinds always send their thanks for a 'polite invitation' in the old style, but on this occasion Miss Lydia was obliged to send regrets as well as thanks, as she had not been very well lately, She, I suppose, was the only person in Stowel who did not accept Mrs. Taylor's invitation. Two parties are, of course, never given on the same day, and it would be considered eccentric to prefer staying at home to going out.

'I am sorry Miss Lydia cannot come,' said Mr. Taylor, when the notes of acceptance were being opened at breakfast-time; 'after all, it is not every day that people have a chance of meeting so distinguished a man as the General.'

'Miss Lydia was never intrusive,' said Mrs. Taylor.

Mrs. Lovekin was one of those who avoided the difficulty raised by Mrs. Taylor's unusual form of invitation, by meeting her accidentally in the baker's shop, where an assortment of cakes was being ordered for the tea-party, and signifying her intention of coming to tea. 'No need to write, I suppose?' said Mrs. Lovekin lightly, 'as I have met you.' Both Mrs. Taylor and the baker's wife thought it would have been in better taste if Mrs. Lovekin had then withdrawn, instead of remaining in the shop and hearing what was being ordered.

Mrs. Taylor had made up her mind at an early stage in the proceedings, that she would be very firm indeed about the matter of dispensing tea herself in her own house. She would appropriate one teapot, and her daughter should have the other, and not even to shake hands with a late-arriving guest, would they run the risk of letting this badge of office fall into the hands of the co-hostess.

'And if,' said Mrs. Taylor, 'I find that she is appropriating The Uncle too much, I shall not hesitate to remove him, on the plea of introducing him to some other and more important guests.'

It was in church on Sunday that we were first allowed to see The Uncle, and this is only following the usual custom in Stowel. Church on Sunday is, as it were, the public life of the town. After a death, it is customary to wait until the family has appeared in church to pay visits of condolence—not so much to avoid intrusiveness in the first hour of grief, as from a feeling that perhaps the crape mourning will not have arrived. In the same way, if anyone moves into a new house—a very unusual proceeding—we are made aware that the carpets are all down, and the drawing-room curtains are hung, when the new arrivals are seen in their pew on Sunday.

This, also, is accepted as a token that calling may now begin. Mrs. Taylor said afterwards, in describing that first Sunday when The Uncle appeared in Stowel Church, that her heart beat so painfully at the door, that she thought she would have been obliged to turn back. It was a triumphal progress that the party of four made up the centre aisle to their pew, but the inward excitement of the Taylors made a natural deportment difficult. Neither Mrs. Taylor nor her daughter joined in the hymns or the responses that Sunday morning. It is doubtful whether they heard a word of the service.

Sir John is a very military-looking person, with white whiskers and a bald pink head. He sat between Mrs. and Miss Taylor, who supplied him with hymn and prayer books in as natural a manner as they found it possible to assume; and Mr. Taylor sat at the end of the pew, with a genial expression on his face, and a look of tempered pride, due no doubt to the fact that the General was 'one of my wife's people,' and not a blood relation of his own.

It was a disappointment to Mr. Taylor that his own sister, Mrs. Macdonald—widow of a Scotch gentleman, whom the Taylors always talk of as 'The Laird'—was not able to come to this family gathering. But Mrs. Macdonald pleaded spring cleaning as an insuperable objection to leaving home at present.

As Miss Taylor, Mrs. Macdonald used to be one of Stowel's central figures, for she was a lady of considerable means and an indefatigable housekeeper; and Mr. Macdonald was considered to have done well when he took her as his bride to the North.

The Sunday on which the Taylors appeared in church with The Uncle was curiously hot for the time of year. It was very stuffy in church, and Miss Lydia had a slight fainting attack, and had to leave before the service was over. Following the accepted custom in Stowel, my sister called the next day to ask how she did. But even indisposition, usually a matter of solemn pleasure with us, was overshadowed and shorn of its interest by the presence of The Uncle amongst us. Even the Vicar looked keenly at him from the pulpit before his sermon began, but no one except Mrs. Lovekin was forward enough to address the august party as they left the church. Mrs. Lovekin, who always affirmed that she saw no difference in rank, was the very first person in Stowel to shake hands with The Uncle. She overtook the Taylors before they had even reached the gate of the churchyard, and was perforce introduced to their relative, 'who,' Mrs. Taylor said afterwards, 'was almost more cordial than she could have wished him to be; but of course his manners were always perfect,' What annoyed everyone a little in the days that followed, was that Mrs. Lovekin constantly referred to the General as if he had been an old friend. Whereas of course it was well known in what an intrusive way her precedence had been gained. During the week, however, we all had an opportunity of seeing Sir John, for he was marched in triumph up and down the village street regularly twice a day-Miss Taylor even condescended to subterfuge in the matter. For having taken The Uncle as far as the baker's at the end of the town, with a view to continuing the walk into the country at The Uncle's request, she pretended to have forgotten something at the draper's, and marched him down the street again, in the proud knowledge that all eyes, whether from pedestrians or from the interior of shops and houses in the High Street, were turned upon her. The tobacconist, where The Uncle bought some tobacco, gave Miss Taylor quite a sympathetic look as he said: 'Allow me to send it for you, Sir John,' And Miss Taylor said: 'Do allow him to send it, uncle! I am sure that you ought not to carry parcels for yourself.'

On Thursday, when we went to the party, we saw at once that the Taylors meant to make no snobbish distinction between their guests, but that each and everyone of them was to be introduced to The Uncle.

'I am no good at this sort of thing, Mary,' The Uncle said before the party began, 'and I think I will walk over and see Willie Jacobs, and spend the afternoon with him. Mrs. Taylor turned pale at the suggestion. 'It will ruin it!' she said. 'I shall feel as if I had been acting on false pretences.' And though the General remained as he had been requested to do, he showed a most irritating tendency to slip away, and sometimes he was not to be found at the most critical moments. Mrs. Taylor stationed him close to herself in the drawing-room where she received her guests. But at the very moment when she turned round to effect an introduction between him and some particular friend, it was discovered that the General had slipped off to the smoking-room or the tea-room, or was wandering aimlessly about the garden, looking at the flower-beds.

Altogether, that most successful afternoon (and the Taylors really did feel that it had been a success from the very highest point of view) had still some drawbacks to it, which they regret, and always will regret. For instance, when Miss Taylor had been despatched into what the Taylors call the 'grounds' to see 'what The Uncle is doing' (playfully), 'and tell him to come and make himself agreeable,' she had hardly departed to fulfil her mother's request, when Mrs. Lovekin bore down upon the teapot, poured out several of the most distinguished cups of tea, and handed round macaroons as though they were her own. Last of all, as the party was breaking up, and Mrs. Lovekin's vicarious hospitality was therefore at an end, she was actually heard inviting The Uncle to come and call upon her. Even the Miss Blinds, on being told of the incident, admitted that this behaviour on Mrs. Lovekin's part could not be called anything but forward. Miss Lydia could only say, in a sort of sweet distress,' perhaps she did not mean it;' but Miss Blind shook her head vigorously, and said, 'Bad butter, bad butter, bad butter!'

Margaret Jamieson had, of course, been helping to prepare the party, for Margaret Jamieson always helps whenever there is anything to be done. And Eliza, we thought, made a deep impression upon The Uncle by her knowledge of literature, and the perfectly easy and natural way in which, without a moment's preparation, she alluded to the 'atomic theory.'

'Ah! you are one of the Reading Society young ladies that I heard about,' said he. 'Sorry I couldn't do more for you in the way of books, but that's not in my line at all, you know. I was educated at a grammar school, and I never had the advantages that you young people have nowadays.' (Mrs. Taylor thought this statement unnecessary, but reflected that great men often made allusions of this sort.) 'However, if I ever can be of any use to you—getting you an order for reading at the British Museum, or anything of that sort—I hope you will let me know.'

For one brief day the Jamiesons were inclined to teaze Eliza about having made a conquest, but the Taylors would not have any nonsense of that sort for a moment. It made Mrs. Taylor quite nervous to think of such a thing, and she remarked that that was the worst of having distinguished people to stop with one; there was always somebody running after them. Eliza Jamieson, we noticed, was treated with marked coldness by the Taylors for some time afterwards, and Miss Taylor recollected darkly that it was Eliza's suggestion in the first instance, that The Uncle should be consulted on the choice of books for the Reading Society. 'She may,' said Miss Taylor, 'have had an eye on him from the first.'

A purely visionary affair of this sort, however, could not be considered satisfactory or exciting, even by the Jamiesons; and the Taylors' suspicions and anxieties were put on one side for the time being—ousted from their place, as it were—by the very distinct and exciting rumours which have reached us about Maud. Maud has been staying with friends at Hampstead, and has written home in a certain veiled way which is very provoking, but which nevertheless, gives the impression that another man has come to the point, and proposed to Maud Jamieson. Maud seems out of spirits, and has written to say that she is returning, and this makes the sisters think that she must have accepted her present suitor, and is coming home to shed a few natural tears. Eliza, who walked over to tell us the news, voiced The Family's opinion when she said: 'We have quite made up our minds that if Maud has said "Yes" she is to stick to it this time. She is always in a panic directly she has accepted anyone, but we know that it would be the same whoever it was, and doubtless, unless we are firm, she will treat this admirer just as she treated Mr. Reddy and Albert Gore, and the others. Mamma says that she will not have Maud coerced, and I am sure no one wants to coerce her; but why should she always get to a certain point, and then begin to have doubts? It is so unbusinesslike.'

The very next day Maud Jamieson came to tea. She looked well dressed, as usual, and had some pretty spring finery about her—yellow mimosa wreathing a broad hat, and some yellow ribbons about her tasteful dress—but her pretty face looked very white, and Maud fidgeted nervously for half an hour, and then told me I was so sympathetic she would like to ask me something.

'I dare say she said,' that you have heard something about Mr. Evans from The Family?'

I admitted that I had, and then there was a very long pause.

'How is one to know,' said Maud, 'when it is the real thing?'

Another pause. I wished with all my heart that I could have been more helpful to this young lady in such evident distress of mind; but the intricacies of Maud's thoughts are most difficult to follow, and I thought it better to wait until she had given me her entire confidence.

'Little things,' said Maud, 'might annoy one so much if one had always to live with a man. For instance, I do not think I could ever truly love a man who sniffs.'

'Our friend Mrs. Fielden says,' I remarked, 'that a man generally proposes when he has a cold in his head. But I pointed out to her that these statistics do her no credit.'

'Mr. Evans doesn't sniff,' said Maud. 'I was only citing that as an example of what one might find very trying in a companion for life.'

I assented, and could only suggest hopefully the usual Jamieson remedy that such a defect might be cured after marriage.

'But men are so obstinate about some things,' said Maud. 'For instance, suppose a man were well off and of really excellent character, do you think it would matter much if he wore a white watered-silk waistcoat in the evening? Would it, for instance, appear an insuperable objection to most minds?'

I replied that doubtless it was a serious fault, but that I did not consider it an incurable one, and I further remarked, with what I hoped showed a broad and liberal way of looking at things, that all men had their idiosyncrasies. Maud admitted this, and seemed cheered by the reflection; but she pushed the matter further, and said she would like to know what sort of a man I should presume anyone to be who wore a white watered-silk waistcoat.

'If you care for Mr. Evans—' I began, and regretted that one's articulate expression is sometimes behindhand in the matter of conveying the comprehensiveness of the inner working of one's mind—

'I am afraid I care for someone else,' said Maud, bursting into tears.

'Let me see you home,' I said, unable to think of any but this very doubtful method of consolation—still, it seemed unkind to let her go home alone when she had been crying.

On the threshold of the Jamiesons' house, several of The Family were waiting for us, and they drew me into the drawing-room, while by tacit consent it seemed to be understood that Maud should not join in the conclave, but should go straight upstairs and take off her hat.

'Have you persuaded her?' said Eliza.

'I hope you have put a little common sense into her,' said Kate,

James was admitted to family discussions now, and here remarked that he believed that all girls were happier married.

'Though of course,' said Mettie, 'it is a great risk.'

'Did she tell you,' asked Gracie, 'that she cared for someone else?'

I admitted that Maud had said something of the sort. And her family exclaimed triumphantly that this was always Maud's plea for releasing herself from an engagement, as soon as that engagement had been made.

Mrs. Jamieson remarked that she would not like any of the girls to feel that they were not welcome at home, and all her affectionate daughters kissed her in turn, or patted her hand, and said that they knew that such a thought as wanting to get rid of one of them would never enter her head.

Mrs. Jamieson here left the room to seek her banished daughter and to administer comfort, and the members of The Family conclave said that they hoped that Mrs. Jamieson did not think that they had been unkind.

'If it had not happened so often!' sighed Eliza, 'However, as we do not know Mr. Evans, he can't ask to come down and stay with us, as Mr. Reddy did, so as to have an opportunity of pressing his suit.'

'He cried so much one afternoon,' said Kate, turning in an explanatory sort of way to Mr. Ward, 'that I really thought I should have to send for mamma.' James looked sympathetic, and Grade added: 'We all really felt quite relieved when- he got engaged to someone else three weeks afterwards, and we hear that they are most happy, and have got a dear little baby.'

CHAPTER IX

MRS. FIELDEN'S motor car is still a matter of absorbing interest to the inhabitants of Stowel. When it breaks down, as it frequently does, there is always a crowd round it immediately. Our friends and neighbours in the town have an ingenuous respect for anything that costs a great deal of money, and they are quite congratulatory to anyone who has been for a drive with Mrs. Fielden, and they talk about the motor and its owner, and who has seen it, and who has not, over their afternoon tea.

The motor car is a noisy, evil-smelling vehicle of somewhat rowdy appearance, which leaves a trail behind it as of a smoking lamp. It drew up at our door to-day, and kicked and snorted impatiently until we were ready to get into it. The next moment, with a final angry snort and plunge, it started down the drive and whizzed through the village and up the hill on the other side without pausing to take breath.

'The worst of a motor car is,' said Mrs. Fielden, 'that one gets through every-thing so quickly. In London I get my shopping done in about a quarter of an hour, and then I take a turn round Regent's Park, and I find I have put away about ten minutes, so I fly down to Richmond, and even then it is too early to go to tea any-where. Talking of tea—isn't everybody very hungry? I am really ravenous—and that is the motor car's fault, too. Because one has learned to want one's meals by the amount of business one has got through, and when one has done a whole after-noon's work in three-quarters of an hour, one is dying for tea, just as if it were five o'clock.'

'I have always been ravenous since I was in South Africa, said one of Mrs. Fielden's Colonels, who had driven over in the motor car to take care of her and to bring us back. 'I don't know when I shall satisfy the pangs of hunger which I acquired on the veldt.'

'I think I shall call on Mr. Ellicomb,' said Mrs. Fielden. 'I believe he has ex-cellent afternoon teas, and he is making me an enamel box which I should like to see.'

Ellicomb said once or twice, as we sat in his picturesque house with its blue china and old brass work, that he only wished we had given him warning that we were coming. We found him with an apron on, working at his enamels, and when he had displayed this work to us, he showed us his book-binding, and his fretwork carving, and his type-writing machine. Afterwards we had tea, which Ellicomb poured very deftly into his blue cups, having first warmed the teapot and the cups, and flicked away one or two imaginary specks of dirt from the plates with what ap-peared to be a small lace-trimmed dinner-napkin.

Mrs. Fielden began to admire his majolica ware, of which she knows nothing whatever, and Ellicomb took her for a tour round his rooms, and asked her to guess the original uses of his drain-tiles and spittoons and copper ham-pots. Afterwards we were taken into a very small conservatory adjoining his house, where every plant was displayed to us in turn, and we were subsequently shown his coal-cellar and his larder and his ash-pit before we were allowed to return to the house.

Ellicomb smiles more often than any other man I know, and he had only one epithet to apply to his house. 'It's so cosy,' he said. 'Isn't it cosy?' 'I do think it's a cosy little place.'

Mrs. Fielden was charmed with everything, and deprecated the idea that she might consider the little house very small after Stanby.

'I always think,' she said, 'that I should much prefer to live in a place like this, and then the people who come to see one really would pay one a little attention, instead of talking of nothing but the house.'

The Colonel laughed and apologized.

'Oh, I know I'm not half good enough for Stanby,' said Mrs. Fielden, smiling. 'But I really can't help it! I was brought up in a house with hot and cold water up-stairs, and white paint, and I suppose I never can really appreciate anything else.'

The dignity of Mrs. Fielden's surroundings has never affected her in the very smallest degree, and I do not believe that the traditions of the house interest her in the very least. I am quite aware that she asked me to write out the history of Lady Hylda, for instance, simply because it is part of her charm always to ask one to do something for her. It is the fashion to wait upon Mrs. Fielden's behests, and it would appear almost an unkindness to her many men friends if she did not give them some commission to do when they go up to town. Her manner of thanking one for a service is almost as pretty as her manner of asking it, and I am really not surprised that she is the most popular woman in the country-side.

Mr. Ellicomb said ecstatically that the dim twilight at Stanby was one of the most impressive things he knew, and he added, with a shudder, that he always expected to see ghosts there.

Mrs. Fielden does not believe in ghosts except on those occasions when she has someone very charming to defend her, and she spends her evenings in a cheerful white boudoir in the modern part of the house.

Having admired all the majolica plates in the house, and having completely bewildered her host by showing an interest in him and his possessions one minute, and complete indifference the next, Mrs. Fielden relapsed into one of those little silences which are so characteristic of her. Her silence is one of the most provoking things about her. She has been witty and amusing the moment before, and then relapses into silence in the most natural manner possible, and her face takes a certain wistful look, and a man wonders how he can comfort her or whether he has offended her.

'I think we ought to go now,' she said, coming out of this wistful reverie like a child awaking from sleep. 'Is everyone ready?'

We got into the motor car again and sped onwards along the smooth white road. Every turn made a picture which I suppose an artist would love to paint. There were red-roofed cottages smothered in orchards of plum blossoms, and simple palings set across gaps in the hedges, with gardens beyond, filled with spring flowers. Now a labourer, gray-coated and bent with age, passed by like a flash, as he tramped slowly homewards from his work, and some school-children, loitering to pick primroses under a hedge, dropped their slates and satchels in the ditch, and called to each other to take care, as they clung together and shouted 'Hurrah!' as we passed.

The park gates of Stanby are lion guarded and of stone, and then a long carriage-drive takes one up to the house. The park round the old gray pile was starred with primroses, and ghost-like little lambs were capering noiselessly in the fields. The scent of wallflowers was blown to us from a great brown ribbon of them round the walls of the lodgekeeper's house as we swung through the gates. The sheep in the park, bleating to their young, drew away from the palings where they had been rubbing their woolly sides, and made off to the further corner of the field, and Mrs. Fielden's gray pony in the paddock tossed his heels in a vindictive fashion at us at a distance of fifty yards or more. And the motor car drew up with a jerk at the great doors of the house.

Stanby is not quite so large now as it originally was, immense though the house undoubtedly is, and only some ruins on the north side show where the chapel used to stand. A mound within the ruin's walls marks the resting-place of Hylda—Hylda, whose history I wrote out at the request of Mrs. Fielden, and sent to her; but I don't suppose she has ever read it.

The evening of our arrival at Stanby it pleased Mrs. Fielden to put on an old-fashioned dress of stiffest brocade, which she had found in some old chest in the house. She wore a high comb of pearls in her dark hair, and she looked a very regal and beautiful figure in the great dining-hall and drawing-rooms of her house. She did not play Bridge, as the others did, but sat on a great high-backed chair near my sofa, and told me some of the old stories of the house, and asked me to write down some of them for her.

'I sent you the story of Hylda more than a week ago,' I said, 'and I don't suppose you ever read it.'

'I did read it,' said Mrs. Fielden gently, 'and I liked it very much.'

She had put on an unapproachable mood with her beautiful stiff brocade gown, and the gentleness of her voice seemed to heighten rather than to lessen her royalty. The radiance and the holiday air, which are Mrs. Fielden's by divine right, were not dimmed to-night, so much as transformed. There was a subtle aromatic scent of dried rose-leaves clinging to the old brocade dress, and about herself a sort of fragrance of old-world dignity and beauty. The pearl comb in her hair made her look taller than usual.

A deerhound got up from his place by the fireplace and came and laid his head on her lap, and some footmen in old-fashioned bright blue liveries came in to arrange the card-tables and hand round coffee. Everything was stately and magnificent in the house.

'And you pretend,' I said, 'that you do nothing; yet probably the whole ordering of this house devolves upon you.'

'I am quite a domestic person sometimes,' said Mrs. Fielden.

'It is rather bewildering,' I said, 'to find that you are everything in turn.'

And the next morning she wore a short blue skirt with a silver belt round her waist, and spent the morning punting on the lake with Anthony Crawshay.

'I hope I look after you all properly,' she said at lunch-time, in a certain charming deprecatory way she has of speaking sometimes. 'There really are punts, and horses, and motor cars, and things, if you want them. Will you all order what you like?'

Each man at the table then offered to take Mrs. Fielden for a ride, or a drive, or a row, and not one of them could be quite sure that she had refused to go with him.

'I want to go for a turn in the garden and talk about books,' she said to me as we left the dining-room. And then I found that I was sitting in her boudoir with her having coffee, and that everyone else was excluded from the room—how it was done I have not the slightest idea—and that by-and-by we left the room by the open French windows, and were strolling in the garden in the spring sunshine. The garden, with its high walls, is sheltered from every wind that blows, and there are wide garden-seats in it painted white, and every border was bright with early spring flowers.

'I call this my Grove of Academe,' said Mrs. Fielden.

'Why?'

'Because I think it has a nice classical sound; and it is here I come with my friends and discuss metaphysics.'

'It seems to me you have a great many friends,' I said.

'I was thinking,' said Mrs. Fielden thoughtfully, 'of adding another to their number.'

'I have a constitutional dislike to worshipping in crowded temples,' I said.

Mrs. Fielden became silent.

It would be forging a sword against themselves, did men allow women to know what a powerful weapon silence is. A soft answer turneth away wrath, but a woman's silence makes a man's heart cry out: 'My dear, did I hurt you? Forgive me!'

At the end of five minutes or so of silence, Mrs. Fielden turned towards me and smiled, and the garden seemed to be filled with her. There was no room for anything else but her and that bewildering smile she gave me.

'How is the diary getting on?' she said.

'The diary,' I answered, 'continues to record our godly, righteous, and sober life—'

'Oh,' said Mrs. Fielden quickly, 'don't you think it is possible to be too good sometimes? That is really what I wanted to say to you—I brought you into the garden to ask you that.'

'It is an interesting suggestion,' I remarked, 'and I think we ought to give it to Eliza Jamieson for one of her discussions.

'I do not wish to discuss it with Eliza Jamieson,' said Mrs. Fielden, 'but with you. You know there really is a great danger in becoming too good, for although I do not think that you would grow wings, or hear passing bells, or anything of that sort; still, you might become a little dull, might you not?'

'I don't think it would be possible to become duller than I am,' I replied. 'You have more than once told me that I am not amusing. So long as my sister is not aware of the fact, I do not in the least mind admitting that I find every day most horribly tedious. I suppose I shall get accustomed to it in time, but I don't enjoy being an invalid.'

'You have watched the Jamiesons making flannel petticoats for the poor,' went on Mrs. Fielden, 'and you have had the Curate to tea, and you have been to the Taylors' party, and if it does not kill you, I am sure you will become like people in those books which one gives as prizes to choir-boys.'

'One so often mistakes monotony for virtue,' I said. 'I believe I was beginning to think that there was almost a merit in getting accustomed to a sofa and a crutch.'

'Oh, but it is a sin!' exclaimed Mrs. Fielden. 'It is a sin to get accustomed to anything that is disagreeable. But that is what comes of studying philosophy!'

'I suppose reasoning is always bad,' I said humbly.

'Yes,' said Mrs. Fielden; 'and it is so unnatural, too.'

'I heard a man say the other day,' I said, 'that solitude is always sententious. And he pointed out that foreigners, who are never alone, base their ethics upon conduct; but that English people, who simply do not understand the life of the boulevards and cafes and family affection, sit apart in the solitude of their garrets or studies, and decide that the right or the wrong of a thing consists in what they think about it.'

Then I recollected that this garden was the Grove of Academe, and that it was here that Mrs. Fielden discussed metaphysics with all her friends. 'What cure do you propose?' I said shortly.

'Why not go to London for a little while and enjoy yourselves?' said Mrs. Fielden. 'Put off the conventionalities of Stowel, as the Miss Traceys do, and do something amusing and gay?'

'Did you ever hear of the man in the Bastille,' I said, 'who had been in prison so long, that when he was offered his freedom he elected to remain where he was?'

'But you must break out of the Bastille long before it comes to that!' said Mrs. Fielden. 'Couldn't you do something exciting? I am sure nothing else will restore your moral tone.'

'How is it to be done?' I asked. 'We must recognise the limitations of our environment.'

'You are going to be philosophical,' said Mrs. Fielden; 'you are going to quote Protagoras, or Pythagoras, or Plato, which will not convince me in the least. Philosophy tries to make people believe that things are exactly the reverse of what they are. I don't think that alters the sum total of things very much. Because, by the time that you have proved that all agreeable things are disagreeable, and all unpleasant things are pleasant, you are in exactly the same position as you were before. I dare say it fills up people's time to turn everything upside down and stand everything on its head, but it is not amusing.'

'What do you want me to do?' I asked.

'Couldn't you enjoy yourselves a little,' said Mrs. Fielden, putting on her wistful voice.

'As we are in the Grove of Academe, let me point out that the pursuit of pleasure for its own sake was one of the corrupt forms of a decadent epicureanism,' I said sternly.

'I am quite sure it was,' said Mrs. Fielden smiling; 'but we were talking about your visit to London, were we not?'

And so I knew that the thing was settled, and I thought it very odd that Palestrina and I had not thought of the plan before.

'As it is getting cold,' said Mrs. Fielden, 'I am going to be a peripatetic philosopher,' and she rose from the seat where we were sitting, and gave me her hand to help me up, for I am still awkward with my crutch, and then let me lean on her arm as we walked up and down the broad gravel pathway.

'Don't you think,' she began, 'that it is a great waste of opportunity not to be wild and wicked sometimes, when one is very good?'

'I am afraid I do not quite follow you.'

'What I mean is, what is the good of filling up years of curates and Taylors and flannel petticoats, unless you are going to kick them all over some day, and have a good time. You see, if you and Palestrina were not so good, you would always have to pretend to be tremendously circumspect. But it seems such waste of goodness not be bad sometimes.'

'Your argument being,' I said, 'that an honest man may sometimes steal a horse?'

'Yes, that is what I mean,' said Mrs. Fielden delightedly.

'A dangerous doctrine, and one—'

'Not Plato, please,' said Mrs. Fielden.

. . . It ended in our taking a flat in London for some weeks. It was a small dwelling, with an overdressed little drawing-room, and a red dining-room, and a roomy cupboard for a smoking-room.

'Remember, Palestrina,' I said to my sister when we settled down, 'that we are under strict orders to live a very rapid and go-ahead life while we are in London. Can you suggest anything very rowdy which a crippled man with a crutch and a tendency to chills and malaria might undertake?'

'We might give a supper-party,' said Palestrina brilliantly, 'and have long-stemmed champagne-glasses, and perhaps cook something in a chafing-dish. I was reading a novel the other day in which the bad characters did this. I made a note of it at the time, meaning to ask you why it should be fast to cook things in a chafing-dish or to have long-stemmed champagne-glasses?'

When the evening came, Mrs. Fielden dined with us, and she and Palestrina employed themselves after dinner in rehearsing how they should behave. My sister said, in her low, gurgling voice: 'I think I shall sit on the sofa with my arms spread out on the cushions on either side of me, and I shall thump them sometimes, like the adventuress in a play does.'

'Or you might be singing at the piano,' said Mrs. Fielden, 'and then when the door opens you could toss the music aside and sail across the room, and give your left hand to whoever comes in first, and say, "What a bore! you have come!" or something rude of that sort.'

Mrs. Fielden's spirit of fun inspired my quiet sister to-night, and the two women began masquerading in a way that was sufficiently amusing to a sick man lying on a sofa.

'Or you might continue playing the piano,' Mrs. Fielden went on, 'after anyone has been announced. I notice that that is very often done, especially in books written by the hero himself in the first person. "She did not leave the piano as I entered, but continued playing softly, her white hands gliding dreamily over the keys."'

'I shall do my best,' Palestrina answered, 'and I thought of calling all our guests by their Christian names, if only I could recollect what they are.'

'Nicknames would be better,' said Mrs. Fielden. 'We ought to have found out, I think, something about this matter before the night of the party.'

'What shall we do till they arrive?' said Palestrina.

'We must read newspapers and periodicals,' Mrs. Fielden replied, 'and then fling them down on the carpet. There is something about seeing newspapers on a carpet which is certainly untidy, but has something distinctly Bacchanalian about it.'

'I wish I had a red tea-gown,' sighed my sister.

'Or a white one trimmed with some costly furs,' said Mrs. Fielden. 'Almost any tea-gown would do.'

'One thing I will have!' she exclaimed, starting in an energetic manner to her feet. 'I'll turn all the lamps low, and cover them with pink paper shades. Where is the crinkly paper and some ribbon?'

After that we sat in a rose twilight so dim that we couldn't even read the evening newspaper.

'I don't think they need have come quite so early,' I said, as the first ring was heard at the door-bell.

Mrs. Fielden had insisted upon it that one actress at least should be asked. 'What is a supper-party without an actress?' she had said. And Mrs. Travers, at present acting in Mr. Pinero's new play, was the first to arrive.

'I wonder if you know any of our friends who are coming to-night?' said Palestrina. 'We expect Squash Bosanquet and Dickie Fenwick.' Palestrina then broke down, because we had no idea if these two men had ever answered to these names in their lives. Also she blushed, which spoilt it all, and Mrs. Fielden began to smile.

Mrs. Travers came to the party in a very simple black evening gown, and Bosanquet and Charles Fenwick came almost immediately afterwards. Anthony Crawshay was amongst the friends whom we had invited, because, Palestrina said, as we did not seem to know many fast people, we had better have someone who was sporting. There was an artist whom we considered Bohemian, because he wore his hair long, but he disappointed us by coming in goloshes.

Altogether we were eight at supper. There was an attractive menu, and the long-stemmed champagne-glasses were felt to be a distinct challenge to quiet behaviour.

Palestrina thought that if she were going to be really fast she had better talk about divorce, and I heard her ask Anthony in a diffident whisper if he had read any divorce cases lately. Anthony looked startled, and in his loud voice exclaimed: 'Egad! I hope *you* haven't!' Palestrina coloured with confusion, and I frowned heavily at her which made it worse.

Mrs. Travers seemed to have taken it into her head that Palestrina was philan-thropic, and she talked a great deal about factory girls, and Bosanquet talked about methylated ether. What it was that provoked his remarks on this subject I cannot now recall, nor why he discussed it without intermission almost throughout the entire evening, but I have a distinct recollection of hearing him dinning out the phrase 'methylated ether.'

It was, I think, the dullest party that even Palestrina and I have ever given, and I blame Mrs. Fielden for this. Mrs. Fielden refused to be the centre of the room. She became an onlooker at the party which she had planned, and she smiled affection-ately at us both, and watched I think, to see how the party would go off.

The long-stemmed champagne-glasses were hardly used. Several people said to me jocosely, 'How is South Africa?' and to this I could think of no more suitable reply than, 'It's all right.' We longed for even the Pirate Boy to make a little distur-bance. Palestrina whispered to me that she thought I might throw a piece of bread at someone, or do something. But the action she suggested seemed to me to be in too daring contrast to the general tone of the evening; and really, as I murmured back to her, there seemed to be very little point in throwing my bread at a guest who had done me no harm.

'I wish,' she said to me when we returned to the drawing-room,' that I knew some daring little French songs. In books the girl always sings daring little French songs, and afterwards everyone begins to be vulgar and delightful, like those people in "The Christian." I think I'll light a cigarette.' She did so, and choked a little, and then wondered if Thomas would like her to smoke, and threw the cigarette into the fire. The Bohemian, who had travelled considerably, asked for a map, and told us of his last year's journeyings, tracing out the route of them for us on the map with a pin.

And Mrs. Fielden was smiling all the time.

'I suppose,' I said to my sister, when the last guest had departed, and we sat together in the pink light of the drawing-room before going to bed—'I suppose we carry about with us an atmosphere of slowness which it is impossible to penetrate. You are engaged to Thomas, and I am an invalid—'

'But in books,' said Palestrina wistfully, 'men talk about all sorts of things to girls whether they happen to be engaged or not, and they ask them to go to see galleries with them next day, or squeeze their hands. Of course, I should hate it if they did so, but still, one rather expected it. To-night,' she said regretfully, 'no one talked to me of anything but Thomas.'

'Charles Fen wick,' I said, 'who used to be considered amusing, has become simply idiotic since he married. He gave me an exact account of his little boy's sayings; he copied the way he asked for sugar, like the chirruping of a bird. You won't believe me, I know, but he put out his lips and chirped.'

'I remember being positively warned against him,' said Palestrina, 'when I used to go to dances in London.' She sighed, and added: 'Do you think Mrs. Fielden enjoyed it?'

'I think Mrs. Fielden was distinctly amused,' I replied.

'Do you think,' said Palestrina, still in a disappointed tone, 'that the men would have been more—more larky if we had been alone? Mrs. Fielden always looks so beautiful and dresses so well that I think she impresses people too much, and they are all trying to talk to her instead of making a row.'

'I think we may as well go to bed,' I said.

Palestrina rose slowly, and went towards the bell to ring for my man to help me. She lingered for a moment by my chair. 'Yet books say that men require so much keeping in order,' she said sadly. 'I wish people would not write about what does not occur.'

CHAPTER X

THE Jamiesons have taken lodgings in West Kensington, which they describe as being 'most central'—a phrase which I have begun to think means inexpensive, and near a line of omnibuses. George and the Pirate are assiduous in taking their sisters to the Play, and other places of amusement, and are showing them something of London with a zeal which speaks much for their goodness of heart. Even Mrs. Jamieson has been out once or twice, and although doubly tearful on the morning following any little bit of dissipation, her family feel that the variety has been good for her. Eliza has found that London is radio-active, hence enjoyable. And Eliza had only been once to the Royal Institution when she said it! Maud's engagement to the Hampstead young man has been finally broken off, and Maud has cried so much that her family have forgiven her. Maud explains that it is such an upset for a girl to break off an engagement, and The Family say soothingly that she must just try and get over it.

'We hope,' said Kate, that next time things will arrange themselves more happily, and at least we can all feel that Maud might have married many times, had she wished to do so.' There seems to be a strong feeling in The Family that Maud will go on having opportunities. Arguing from the general to the particular, they have proved, with a sort of tribal feeling of satisfaction, that Maud is undoubtedly very attractive to men, and that if one man likes her, why should not another?

Still, we all felt that we could not have sympathized immediately with another love affair of Maud's, and it was refreshing, not to say most pleasing and surprising, to find that since their arrival in Town, it was Margaret who attracted the notice of a gentleman, Mr. Swinnerton by name, a friend of George's, who brought him to supper one Sunday evening. The Jamiesons could see at a glance, that Mr. Swinnerton was 'struck,' and as he called two or three times in the following week, Margaret made the usual Jamieson opportunity of seeing Palestrina home, one afternoon when she had been to call, to embark in confidences about her lover, in the usual Jamieson style. Margaret is diffident, bashful, shy, uncertain about Mr. Swinnerton's feelings for her, and hopelessly nervous lest her family should have had their expectations raised only to be disappointed. She implored Palestrina over and over again to say nothing about it to them, though it has been more than obvious to us all along how full of expectation every member of The Family is. It was a very wet evening as Margaret and my sister left the Jamiesons' lodgings, but she hardly seemed conscious of the inclemency of the weather, and begged Palestrina not to think of taking a cab, as she particularly wished to speak to her.

'At first,' she began, 'I thought it must be Maud, although she has but just broken off her engagement to Mr. Evans; still, one knows she is the pretty one, and if anyone calls often, it is generally her.'

It was a little difficult to follow Margaret's rapid, ungrammatical speech, but Palestrina and I both knew that to the vigorous minds of the Jamiesons, there must be a direct purpose in every action, and that therefore if Mr. Swinnerton came to call, he must have a purpose, presumably a matrimonial purpose, for paying his visits. After two or three afternoon calls from a gentleman, the Jamiesons generally ask each other ingenuously, 'Which of us is it?' It hardly seems to them respectable that a man should continue to pay them visits, unless he means to show a prefer- ence for one of them.

Presuming that it was not Maud he came to see, Margaret, with modest hesita- tion and many blushes, asked Palestrina if she did not think it possible that these visits might be intended for her.

'Please do not say anything about it to the others. I always have so hoped that if ever I had a love affair, it would be when I was away from home. Do you know at all what they think about it?'

She did not pause for a reply, but began again: 'You see he has called three times in one week, but' (hopelessly), 'I am always surrounded by The Family, and he couldn't say anything if he wanted to. Of course I don't think it has come to anything of that sort yet; still, you know, we could get to know each other better if there were not so many of us always about. Maud doesn't mind a bit; she has had love affairs in front of us all, and she does not mind talking about them in the least, or even asking us to let her have the drawing-room to herself on certain af- ternoons. But I don't feel as if I could bear to have this discussed before anything is settled. And then we have so few opportunities. Maud generally takes them to a distant church, and then they have the walk home together. But I never quite know whether she makes the suggestion about church, or if she merely thinks it would be nice, and leaves the man to make it.'

'Maud,' I remarked parenthetically to Palestrina, 'has raised love-making to a science—an exact science.'

I hope you don't think for a moment,' Margaret had gone on, 'that I am abusing Maud; you know how fond we all are of each other.'

Maud's experiences on matters matrimonial are always quoted as precedent in the Jamieson family, and she is cited whenever anything of the sort is afoot. Each phase in her experience is frankly discussed, and conclusions are drawn from it; and I have heard the Jamiesons say,' Mr. So-and-so must be in love with Miss So-and-so, he looks at her in exactly the same way that Mr. Reddy used to look at Maud.' Maud herself, unconsciously, as I believe, makes a sort of calendar of her love affairs, and it is quite usual for her to date an event by referring to it as having happened 'in the Albert Gore days,' or 'when Mr. Evans was hovering.'

Margaret's voice had not ceased from the moment they left the lodgings together. 'It is, however, no use trying to copy other people in your love affairs,' she said, 'because it seems to come to everyone so differently, and then of course, different people must call forth different feelings. I don't think I could have felt for Mr. Reddy, for instance, quite as I do now, even if he had been in love with me. You feel so bewildered somehow.'

The walk had by this time become very rapid, and Margaret knocked against all the foot-passengers whom she met travelling in the opposite direction, in her short-sighted way. Her umbrella showered raindrops upon Palestrina, and she became so incoherent that my sister suggested taking a cab to our flat, and talking things over quietly when they should get there.

It was about eleven o'clock that night when Margaret Jamieson took leave of us, and by that time I fancy the bridesmaids' dresses had been arranged.

A few days later Palestrina received a note by the hand of a messenger-boy; it bore the word 'Immediate' on the cover, and had evidently been addressed in some haste.

'DEAR PALESTRINA (it ran),

'Can you possibly come to make a fourth at a concert this afternoon? Do come, even if it should be rather inconvenient to you. I want you so much. Mr. Swinnerton has asked mamma and me, and he has taken tickets. They are not reserved places, so we could easily arrange to meet at the door and sit together. Three is such an awkward number. I fear mamma does not care for him, and that is a great grief to me. I will tell you everything this afternoon.

'Yours affectionately, 'MARGARET JAMIESON.

'P.S.—It is all going to come right, I believe, but I have had immense difficulties. Hardly ten minutes alone with him—you know we have only one sitting-room—but the family have been sweet.'

Hugo,' said Palestrina,' this is an occasion when you could give very substantial aid to a deserving family.'

'I am sorry I am engaged this afternoon,' I said, with an instinct of self-preservation, without however having any definite idea of what Palestrina might say next.

'It is I who am engaged this afternoon,' said my sister smiling, 'and you are perfectly aware of that fact. Thomas is taking me down to Richmond to introduce me to his aunt. Besides, Hugo, you know you like music'

'I am very sorry, Palestrina,' I said, 'but it is quite impossible.'

'Margaret is the Jamieson you like best,' said Palestrina, 'and I hate to think of your being here alone a whole afternoon. What were you thinking of doing?'

I had been thinking of going to this concert, and Palestrina guessed it, of course.

. . .

I was at the door of the concert hall at two-thirty in the afternoon, and found Mrs. Jamieson and Margaret and the young man already on the pavement, looking as if they had stood there for a considerable time. Mr. Swinnerton is a large, rather stupid-looking man, with a red face, a crooked nose, and curly hair. He wore a dark blue overcoat, so thick and strong that it reminded one of some encasement of plaster of Paris, or of some heavy coat of mail. His hands were covered by yellow dog skin gloves, equally unyielding, so that Mr. Swinnerton appeared deprived of any agility of movement by his garments. Mr. Swinnerton is in the volunteers, and has 'Captain Swinnerton' printed on his cards. He gave me the idea of seeming to think that every action of his was some epoch-making event, and he frequently referred during the afternoon to having seen a picture then on view at one of the galleries, as though this were rather an up-to-date, not to say remarkable, proceeding. Margaret seemed a good deal impressed by his manner, and the Jamiesons had decided that he was 'smart,' which was a further and quite unnecessary addition to Mr. Swinnerton's vanity, and very bad for a gentleman of his complacent character.

He ushered us into the Queen's Hall in an important sort of way, which gave one the impression that the place belonged to him; and the fact that I was making a third in a party under his guidance, convinced me that I was in some sort adding to his self-satisfaction. Mr. Swinnerton had chosen shilling places, because, as he informed us a great number of times, these were in the best position for hearing the music. Mrs. Jamieson was disappointed. In her class of life, a treat is given on a more magnificent scale.

'Shall I sit next you, Mrs. Jamieson?' I said, for I believed that this was what I was intended to say; but Mr. Swinnerton remarked to Margaret, 'I'll go next; I like to divide myself amongst the ladies.'

Mrs. Jamieson looked uncomfortable in the small amount of space a shilling had procured for her, and she suggested apologetically that she would like a programme; but the music was beginning, and Mr. Swinnerton put up his large, stiff-gloved hand like a slab, and said, 'Hush!'

We went faithfully through the orthodox Queen's Hall concert from the very first note, to the 'Ride of the Valkyries,' and after every item on the programme our host turned to us, moving his whole body in his stout coat, and said, 'Isn't that nice now—very nice I call it!' still with an air of ownership.

Mrs. Jamieson slept a little; but the hardness of her seat formed an uneasy resting-place, and it is to be feared that her mantle with the storm collar was too hot; but, she whispered to me in a burst of confidence, she was unable to remove it, owing to the fact that the bodice and skirt of her dress did not correspond.

I always like these places,' said Mr. Swinnerton again, 'they are exactly in the centre of the hall, and another thing is, they are near the door in case of fire,'

Margaret assented sweetly. I always thought until to-day that Margaret Jamieson was a plain woman; to-day I find she is good looking.

'It is ridiculous,' said Mr. Swinnerton, 'to see the way people throw their money away on really inferior seats, just because they think they are fashionable.'

Mrs. Jamieson stirred a little on her uneasy bench, and Mr. Swinnerton said, in self-defence, 'Don't you agree with me, eh?'

'I think,' said Mrs. Jamieson politely, 'that perhaps for a long concert the *fotoys* would be more comfortable.'

'Ah!' cried Mr. Swinnerton, you want to be fashionable, I see; but there are many of the best people who come to these seats. I know of a Member of Parliament—I don't know him, I know of him' (we felt that some connection with the Member had been established)—'who comes regularly to these very places, and who declares they are the best in the house.'

'Perhaps,' said Mrs. Jamieson simply, 'he had never tried the *fotoys.*'

After the concert was over, Mr. Swinnerton suggested that Margaret and her mother should go and have tea at a bun-shop, qualifying the suggestion with the remark, ' I know you ladies can never get on without afternoon tea.' When with Mr. Swinnerton, ladies are never allowed to forget that he is a gentleman and they are ladies, and that a certain. forbearance is therefore extended to them. He offered his arm to Mrs. Jamieson, who gathered up her skirt and umbrella in one hand, and accepted the proferred support in some embarrassment. Margaret fell behind with me, and whispered in a sort of excited way:

'Hasn't it been lovely? Do tell me what you think—I mean about him?'

'I haven't had much chance of judging,' I replied stupidly; 'but he seems ail right, although perhaps his ideas are not very large.'

'Still, you mean that one could always alter that,' said Margaret quickly, with the true Jamieson optimism, as applied to the beneficial results of matrimony. There is hardly, I believe, a defect that they think they will not be able to eradicate in a future husband, save perhaps, the conical shape of Mr. Ward's head. 'But I really do not think that there is anything .that I would like altered,' she added simply.

'His name is Tudor,' she went on; 'George calls him that now, and Maud is beginning to do so—Maud is being so kind, she says it promotes a familiar tone which is very helpful, to call him "Tudor," but I can't call him anything but Mr. Swinnerton yet.'

After tea, Mr. Swinnerton asked us how we had enjoyed our entertainment, and Margaret expressed herself in the highest terms in praise of it. There seemed to be a lingering tendency on Mrs. Jamieson's part, to revert to the superior comfort of seven-and-sixpenny places and arm-chairs, but we checked this by saying with emphasis that it was a friendly afternoon of this kind that we really enjoyed. Mr. Swinnerton then put the Jamiesons into an omnibus, and directed the conductor to Met these ladies out at the top of Sloane Street,' in a tone of voice that suggested that they were to be caged and padlocked until that place of exit was reached. He lifted his hat with a fine air to them, and then, as I had called a hansom, he put me into it rather elaborately, and cautioned the commissionaire at the door to 'take care of this gentleman.'

He will probably call me a South African hero next; I wish he would keep his attentions to himself.

CHAPTER XI

LAST night we dined at the Darcey-Jacobs'. Mrs. Darcey-Jacobs is 'enjoying one breath of life' at a hotel with the Major, and she has left quite a pathetic number of visiting-cards on all her friends, so that her short London season may be as full of gaiety as possible. Neither of us looked forward to the dinner-party being particularly lively, but we were a good deal amused at the turn the conversation took during dinner. I have often thought since, that a certain dumbness which falls upon some entertainments, can be dispersed if the subject of matrimony is started, and I will class with it a discussion on food, and on personal experience at the hand of the dentist. Any of these three subjects can be thrown, as it were, into the stagnant deep waters of a voiceless party, and the surface will be instantly rippled with eager conversation.

Talk flagged a little in the private sitting-room of the hotel where the Darcey-Jacobs' gave their dinner-party. Major Jacobs, in his guileless way, gave us an exhaustive list of the friends whom they had invited for that evening, but who had not been able to come, and this had a curious depressing effect upon us all, and within ourselves we speculated unhappily as to whether we had been asked to fill up vacant places.

'Why are men always allowed to blunder?' said Mrs. Darcey-Jacobs, looking over her high nose at the gentleman next her, and tapping him on the arm with her lorgnettes.

Major Jacobs, from his end of the table, looked penitent but mystified.

'Happy is the woman,' said Mrs. Darcey-Jacobs, 'who has no men about her.'

'I should like to have been born a widow,' said a pretty girl with beseeching blue eyes and a soft, confiding expression, who sat a little lower down on my side of the table. And then the subject of matrimony was in full swing.

'Marriage is just an experience,' said a shrill-voiced American widow, who sat opposite. 'Everyone should try it, but that is no reason why one should not be thankful when it is over.'

'I am much interested in what you say,' said Mrs. Darcey-Jacobs, with a certain profound air suitable to so great a subject. One felt the want of the Jamiesons sadly during the ensuing discussion, and I almost found myself, in the words of Mettie, making the suggestion that marriage was a great risk.

'Someone once said,' ventured Major Darcey-Jacobs, 'that choosing a wife was like choosing a profession—it did not matter much what your choice was, so long as you stuck to it; it was a mere figure of speech, no doubt—'

'I hope so, indeed,' said Mrs. Darcey-Jacobs.

'Marriage is the worst form of gambling,' broke in an elderly gentleman; 'it should be suppressed by law. Talk about lotteries! Talk about sweepstakes! Why, the worst you can do, if you put your money into them, is to draw a blank. Now, this is fair play, I consider; you either get a prize or you get nothing. But matrimony, sir, is a swindle, compared with which the Missing Word Competition appears like a legal document beside a forged banknote.'

If the old gentleman had a wife present, she was evidently of a callous disposition, for I saw no wrathful expression on any face.

Mr. Ellicomb—even in London, Ellicomb and Anthony Crawshay are asked to meet us—gave it as his opinion that a woman's hand was wanted in the home. The voice was the voice of Ellicomb, the sentiment was the sentiment of Maud, and Palestrina and I very nearly exchanged glances.

After this, several people began to describe at one and the same time, in quite a breathless way, their own personal experiences of the happiness of wedded life.

'Of course,' said Major Darcey-Jacobs, 'a good deal of forbearance must be exercised if married life is to be a success. And Mrs. Darcey-Jacobs said quickly: 'I hope you do not intend to become personal, William.' To which William replied that no such intention had been his.

Anthony said in his cheery voice: 'Of course it is give and take, don't you know, and then it is all right.'

Everyone volunteered ideas on the subject—not once, but several times. And those who applauded the happy state, shouted each other down by quoting examples of wedded bliss in such words as: 'Look at Hawkins!' 'Look at Jones!' 'Look at the Menteiths!'

Quite suddenly Mrs. Darcey-Jacobs leaned across the table, smiled at her husband, and remarked: 'Look at us, William!'

I do not think I have ever seen anyone look so astonished as Major Jacobs. 'That was very pretty of Maria,' he said, in a low voice; 'very pretty of her, by Gad!' And we caught him looking at his wife several times that evening with a puzzled but delighted expression on his face.

After dinner we played Bridge. 'I disapprove of the game myself,' said Mrs. Darcey-Jacobs, who certainly was the worst player I have ever met, 'but Mrs. Fielden likes it, and she has promised to come in the evening.'

Mrs. Fielden arrived at the same time as Colonel Jardine, and they played as partners together, with me and the American widow as opponents. Colonel Jardine wore some kind of lead ring on his finger, which he said cured gout, and gathered up his tricks in a stiff sort of way. He had a pet name for almost every card in the pack, and he babbled on without once ceasing throughout the rubber. 'Now we'll see where old Mossy Face is. I think that draws the Curse of Scotland. Kinky takes that,' and so on. It was perfectly maddening, but Mrs. Fielden seemed quite pleased. I don't suppose she ever feels irritated. The American widow, who was my partner, was only just learning the game. When I said to her, 'May I play?' she always replied, if she had a bad hand, 'No, certainly not,' And when it was pointed out to her that she had either to say, 'If you please,' or 'I double,' she replied, 'Don't ask me if you may play, if you mean to do it whether I like it or not.' She always gave us such items of information as 'I know what I should say if it was left to me this time,' and she frequently doubled with nothing at all in her hand, because she said she liked to play a plucky game.

I have tried to cure Mrs. Fielden of saying 'dahmonds' when she means 'diamonds,' but it is quite useless. She also says (with a radiant smile) 'How tarsome!' when she has lost a rubber, although I have pointed out to her that that is not the phonetic pronunciation of the word. When we are all wrangling over the mistakes and misdeeds of the last round, Mrs. Fielden looks hopelessly at us and says, 'Is it anyone's deal? And then we laugh and stop arguing. She never keeps the score, or picks up the cards, or deals for herself, or does anything useful.

The American widow did not stop talking most of the time, and the Colonel kept up his running commentary upon the cards he was playing, and then Mrs. Darcey-Jacobs joined us to look on, and she and the American widow plunged into a discussion on clothes, which they kept up vigorously all the time. This necessitated a number of questions relating to the game from the American widow, when-ever she was recalled to the fact that she was playing Bridge: 'May I see that laast trick? What's trumps? Does my hand go down on the table this time?' Mrs. Fielden beamed kindly upon her, even when the widow had debated five minutes which card to lead, and Colonel Jardine had begun to play the chromatic scale of impa-tience up and down the table with his stiff fingers.

'Waal,' said the American widow to Mrs. Fielden, 'I think you are just lovely, and I would like to play with you always. I believe most people would like to kill me at Bridge. Caan't think why. Colonel Jardine, did you play the lost chord?'

'I know the tune,' said the Colonel; 'but I don't play at all.'

The American turned bewildered eyes upon Mrs. Fielden, who said, smiling: 'Colonel Jardine is practising the chromatic scale. I think he will be a very good player some day.'

'How was I to know,' said the Colonel, spluttering over his whisky-and-soda when the American widow had left, 'that she meant the last card? That woman would drive me crazy in six weeks.'

'I liked her,' said Mrs. Fielden, 'and she is very pretty.'

There is a certain large-heartedness about this pretty woman of fashion and of the world, which constrains her to say something kind about everyone. With her, the absent are always right, and I do not think I have ever heard her say an unkind word about anyone. At Stanby, when people who are staying there make a newly-departed guest run the gauntlet of criticism—not always of the kindest sort—Mrs. Fielden says, in that royal fashion of hers which makes her approval the final deci-sion in all matters, 'I liked him.' And the departed guest's character and reputation are safe. Her charity is boundless and quite indiscriminate, save that she sends a trifle more rain and sunshine on the unjust than on the just.

'Come to lunch with me some day,' she said to me in the off-hand way in which she generally gives an invitation. 'I am always at home at two o'clock. Why not come to-morrow? You are leaving town almost immediately, are you not?'

Mrs. Darcey-Jacobs is also asked to lunch; everyone is asked to lunch. When one goes to the pretty widow's house in South Street, one generally finds a dozen people lunching with her.

. . . She came into the room—late, of course—and found ten or twelve people waiting for lunch. 'I am so sorry I Do you all know each other?' she asked of the rather constrained group of strangers making frigid conversation to each other in the flower-filled drawing-room. And then she began to introduce us to each other, and forgot half our names, and we were downstairs in a buzz of conversation and laughter, and filled with something that is odd and magnetic which only comes when Mrs. Fielden arrives.

As is always the way at her lunch-parties, her carriage drives up to the door before anyone has finished coffee, and then we all say good-bye, complaining of the rush of London.

'I want you to drive with me this afternoon,' said Mrs. Fielden, when I with the others was saying good-bye. I think she generally singles somebody out for a drive or a long talk, or to take her to a picture-gallery after lunch, and it is done in a way that makes the one thus singled out feel foolishly elated and flattered.

'I think we are going to drive down to Richmond and see some trees and grass, and behave in a rural sort of way this afternoon,' she announced, as she seated herself in the carriage.

'And what about all your engagements for this afternoon?' I asked. 'And the Red Book, and the visiting list, and the shopping list, and the visiting cards, which I see with you?'

'I never keep engagements,' said Mrs. Fielden; 'and everyone knows my memory is so bad that they always forgive me. Someone gave me a little notebook the other day, with my initials in silver upon it—I can't remember who it was—and I put down in it all the tarsome things I ought to do, and then I lost the little pocket-book.'

'If I ever find it,' I said, 'I shall bring it to you, and read out all your tarsome engagements to you.'

'I didn't say "tarsome," ' said Mrs. Fielden.

'I suppose you are whirling through the London season,' I said presently, 'and going everywhere, and having your frocks chronicled in the magazines, and going to a great many parties?'

'No,' said Mrs. Fielden; ' I have been down at Stanby.'

'I wish,' I remarked, 'that you did not always give one unexpected replies. Why have you been down at Stanby? You didn't say anything about it when I saw you last night.'

'Do you know old Miss Lydia Blind?' said Mrs. Fielden. 'She is ill, and I got rather a pathetic letter from her, so I went down to Stanby to look after her.'

She fumbled for the pocket of her dress, raising first what seemed to be a layer of lace, and then a number of layers of chiffon, and then, after rustling amongst some silk to find her artfully-concealed pocket, she produced a letter and handed it to me.

'Am I to read it?' I said; and Mrs. Fielden nodded.

'. . . One so often hears,' so the letter ran, 'of a case of long illness in which the one who is strong, and who acts as nurse to the invalid, breaks down before the end comes. To me it has always seemed to show that the strong one's courage has failed somehow, and that, had zeal been stronger or faith greater, she might have endured to the end. . . .'And, again, in a postscript: 'When I was younger I was very impatient, and I think I could not well have borne it had I known that life was to be a waiting time. I do not say this in any discontented spirit, dear, and I only write to you because you always understand. . . .'And then the letter broke off suddenly, and I handed it back to Mrs. Fielden.

'So this is you, as Miss Lydia knows you,' I said.

'I want you to go and see her when you go back to Stowel. Will you?' said Mrs. Fielden. 'Miss Lydia is an angel, I think; the best woman really that ever lived. Will you take her some things I am sending her, and ask how she is when you go back?'

We drove under the trees of Richmond Park in Mrs. Fielden's big, luxurious carriage. She generally drives in a Victoria, and I asked her why she had the landau out this afternoon.

'A whim,' said Mrs. Fielden. 'I am full of whims.'

But of course a landau is the only carriage in which a lame man, who has to sit with his foot up, can put it comfortably on the opposite seat.

We drove onwards, and she stopped the carriage to look at the view from Richmond Hill, and the soft air blew up to us in a manner very cool and refreshing, and then we got out and walked about for a time, and Mrs. Fielden gave me her arm.

'I don't really require an arm,' I said, 'but I like taking yours.'

'It is a very strong arm,' said Mrs. Fielden; and she exclaimed quickly: 'I believe I am getting fat! My maid tells me all my dresses want altering. I wish it was time to think about beginning to hunt again.

'Do you know,' I said, 'I always thought, till I got back to England, that my leg had been taken off below the knee, and that I should be able to get astride of a horse again. I never used to see it, of course, when they dressed it; and when I counted up the things I should be able to do, riding was always one of them. I didn't sell my horses till just the other day.'

Mrs. Fielden did not sympathize, but one of her silences fell between us. We did not speak again till she began to tell me an amusing story which made us both laugh; but when she was sitting in the carriage, and the footman was helping me in, and we were still laughing, I could have sworn that her eyes looked larger and softer than I have ever seen them.

CHAPTER XII

IT is always rather melancholy arriving at home alone, and I miss Palestrina very much at these times, and I feel ill-disposed towards Thomas. Down-Jock pretended not to know me, and barked furiously when I drove up to the door, and then ran away on three legs, making believe, as he sometimes does when he wants to appeal to one's pity, that he is old and lame.

It was still early in the afternoon, and the sunshine was blazing over everything when I hobbled down the hill to inquire for Miss Lydia. The houses in Stowel are all roofed with red tiles, and each garden has flowering shrubs in it or beds full of bright-coloured flowers, so that the little place has a very warm and happy look on a sunny summer day. A great heavy horse-chestnut tree hung over the walls of the doctor's house, and scattered fragments of pink blossoms when the soft air stirred gently. The wistaria on the post-office was in full bloom. And the place was so full of pleasant sounds this afternoon—of singing birds, and heavy rolling waggons moving up the broad street, and the laughter of children, and the soft rush of the summer wind through the trees, that one felt that a day like this gave one a very strong leaning in favour of the happy view that life is, after all, a good thing.

One had, of course, to stop and speak to several old friends, who said they were thankful to see me back, as though a visit to London were an expedition fraught with many dangers.

When I reached the little cottage with the green gate, and the maid opened the door to me, she told me that Lydia Blind had died an hour ago.

The staircase of the little house is directly opposite the front door. I could not but believe that if I waited a little while Miss Lydia would descend the stairs, as she always did, with a smile which never failed to welcome everyone. Or if she were not within doors, that I would only have to pass out into the little garden at the back of the house to find her. I thought suddenly of the words of a boy I used to know at school, who, when a young playfellow died, said between his sobs: 'It was so hard upon him dying before he had had a good time.' Certainly ever since we knew her, Lydia's life had been one long sacrifice to a witless invalid, and I couldn't help feeling that perhaps no one would ever know the extent of her patient service. Probably there never lived a more unselfish woman, and I cannot think why she never married.

She was a person who lacked worldly wisdom, and in worldly matters she was not prosperous—she never sowed that sort of grain. It was very touching to find that she had not even a few trinkets to leave behind, but that one by one each had been sold to pay for something for the invalid—a doctor's fee, or a chemist's heavy bill. She left the world as unobtrusively as she lived in it. Her last illness was very sudden and brief, and probably she would have been thankful that the little household was spared any extra expense.

The news of Lydia's death was unexpected by every one. When I turned and left the house and was walking home again, I met Mrs. Taylor going to inquire about her neighbour's health, with an offering of fruit in a little basket. She begged me, in the Stowel fashion, to turn and walk back with her, declaring that she felt so seriously upset by the news, that if I would only see her as far as her gate, I should be doing her a kindness. In the garden, the General who had run down to Stowel for a couple of days, was reclining in a deck-chair, Indian fashion. He was reading some cookery recipes in a number of *Truth,* and he turned to his niece, as she crossed the lawn, and said, 'Do you think your cook could manage this, Mary? Select a fine pineapple—'

'Oh, uncle,' said Mrs. Taylor, with a good deal of feeling,' we have had such bad news! Our dear old friend in the village, Miss Lydia Blind, is dead.'

'What Lydia Blind?' said the General; and Mrs. Taylor replied:

'You never knew her, dear. She wasn't able to come to the party; indeed, I think she has been ailing ever since about that time, but we had no idea that the end was so near.'

'It can't be the Lydia Blind I used to know?' said the General.

'Oh no, you couldn't have known her,' said Mrs. Taylor, with a sob; 'she was just a dear old maiden lady living in the village on very small means.'

'She hadn't a sister called Belinda, had she?' said the General.

Mrs. Taylor said she had, and I remembered suddenly how I had seen Lydia Blind standing one morning in front of the General's picture in the photographer's shop, and hearing her say, 'I used to know him.'

Mrs. Taylor went indoors, and I said good-bye, but the General said to me abruptly, 'I should like to see her; will you take me there?' And he did not say more until we found ourselves in the little porch of the cottage. He looked very tall standing by the low door of the house, and an odd idea came to me that Miss Lydia would have been proud of her afternoon caller.

'Let me go alone,' he said gruffly, when he had asked permission to go to her room, and I waited in Lydia's morning-room, with its twine cases and unframed sketches, and the photographs of babies.

'I cannot see the sister,' said the General irritably, when he had rejoined me in the darkened room. 'Is she still dumb, poor thing? If ever there was a case,' he went on, 'of one life—and, to my mind, the sweeter and the better life—being sacrificed to another, it is in the case of Lydia Blind.' He sat down on the little green sofa, and looked about him with eyes that seemed to see nothing. 'I never expected such a thing,' he said;

'I couldn't have expected a thing like this . . . I didn't even know she lived here . . . Do you remember her,' he said, 'when she was very pretty? No, no, of course you wouldn't. . . . It doesn't hurt you to walk a little, does it? I have lived nearly all my life out of doors, and when anything upsets me I cannot stand being within four walls. . . .'

We went out and crossed the field-path into the woods beyond. The paths of the woods are narrow and uneven, and at first we walked in single file, until we came to the broader road beyond the stream, and then we walked on side by side, the General suiting his pace to my slow, awkward gait.

'. . . .Did you ever know the Bazeleys at all? No, you wouldn't, of course; that would be before your time. They had a very pretty place in Lincolnshire—a charming place—with a veranda round the house, and wicker-chairs with coloured cushions on them—more like an Indian house than an English one. . . . Harold Bazeley was in love with Lydia too.' (I believe the General was talking more to himself than to me.) 'It was one night sitting in the veranda that I heard him begin to make love to her for all he was worth, and I had to cut it. . . . Poor chap! he came into the smoking-room that night where I was sitting alone, and he sat down by the table and put his head in his hands. He may have been saying his prayers (for he was always a religious man . . . he did a lot of good for the men under him in India), and I sat with him till it was time to go to bed. I don't know if it was any comfort to him, but I knew from his face that Lydia must have said no, and I thought perhaps he wouldn't like being alone. . . . Well, then of course one didn't like to rush in and ask one's best friend's girl to marry one so soon after his disappointment. One had very strict ideas about honour in those days; I hope one has not lost them. . . . It is very odd that I was never here before, until last spring. Nearly all my service has been abroad, and I generally used to spend my leave hunting or in London, and .my niece used to come up and stay with me there. . . . I didn't care much for Taylor in those days, but he really isn't a bad sort of fellow.'

The sun began to sink behind the trees, and the General seemed to wake from the reverie in which he had been talking to me, and said: 'You oughtn't to be out after sunset, if you have still got malaria about you,' and we began to walk slowly homewards.

'It was just such an evening as this,' he said, 'when I bade her good-bye, meaning to come back in a little while and ask her to marry me. She was standing by the gate—fine old gates with stone pillars to them, and the sun shone full in her eyes. . . . I suppose that gentle, sweet look never left them, did it? They were closed, of course, when I saw them just now. . . . She was wearing a white dress that evening, I remember—a sort of muslin dress which I suppose would not be fashionable now, but which looked very pretty then. It had a lot of pink ribbons about it, and there was a great bunch of pink moss-roses in the ribbon of her belt. . . . Do you know I never picture her except as the girl who stood by the gate with the sun behind her, and the roses in her belt. I think I lost my head a little when it came to saying good-bye, and I began to say things which I had not meant to say—she looked so pretty with the red sunlight upon her, and her white muslin dress almost turned to pink in the glare. . . . I don't think she was surprised, only sweeter and gentler than before, and a curious happy look was in her eyes. But I stopped in time, and stammered like a fool, thinking of poor Harold Bazeley, and then I said good-bye rather hurriedly. But I came back again to the gate where she was still standing, and asked if I might have one of the roses in her belt. And she gave me the whole bunch.

'. . . It must have been after this that the father died and left them very poor, and then the sister (this one, Belinda) had a stroke of paralysis, and there was no one to look after her but Lydia. . . . I wrote and proposed to her before I went to India—asked her to come with me as my wife. But she said she could not marry while her sister lived. It isn't as though we could have remained in England, and she could have lived with us; but of course India would have been an impossibility for the poor thing. We never thought in those days that poor Belinda would live long. And then she made a sort of recovery, but was still quite helpless, and Lydia wrote and asked me to wait for her no longer. . . . I never heard that she had come to live at Stowel.'

The broad, wide village road was dim with twilight when we walked home along it—The Uncle and I. The children had all gone home, and the flowers in the little garden had lost their colour in the dim light.

As we passed by the cottage, the General halted on the quiet, deserted road and took off his hat, then he leaned over the little green paling and drew towards him a branch of a moss-rose tree that Miss Lydia had planted there. He plucked a bud from it and held it to his face. Then he said gently, 'They are the same sort, but they do not smell so sweet.'

CHAPTER XIII

MRS. FIELDEN came to Stowel for the funeral, and did not return to London again. She went to pay some visits, I believe, and afterwards she will go to Scotland to stay with the Melfords, as she always does in August. It was a very quiet summer.

Anthony went to Ireland to fish, and Major Jacobs went with him instead of me: Anthony and I used to take the fishing together. Even Frances Taylor went north to stay with Mrs. Macdonald, and the Reading Society postponed its future meetings till the winter should come again.

Undoubtedly Kate Jamieson's wedding was a stirring event in a very dull time. The festivities connected with it were carried out with the Jamieson's usual energy and lavishness. It is possible to be lavish on five hundred a year. That is one of the pleasing things that kind-hearted people like the Jamieson's can prove. No one was omitted in the list of invitations to the reception which was held on the lawn in front of the house. And there the whole of the Jamiesons' wide circle of friends was gathered together, forming an assembly which surely only the censorious mind could find fault with. The refreshments, these good Jamiesons informed us, with their ingenuous interest in discussing detail, were prepared by Margaret, and Kate contributed to the payment of their ingredients from her small savings. The group of bride and bridesmaids, which was photographed at the front door, each wearing an expression of acute distress upon her face, was George's own idea, and was nobly paid for by him.

It was announced at the wedding-feast—although it had been whispered for a long time—that there was soon to be another break in the Jamieson family, We all instantly prepared a smile of congratulation for Maud, and some disappointment was felt when it was discovered that the remark applied to Mrs. Jamieson's youngest son, Kennie. The Pirate had for some time been informing his friends that the Wild West was 'calling to him,' and that he had the 'go fever,' and that 'once he had known the perfect freedom of life out there' it was impossible to settle down to the conventionalities of English society again. The Pirate had obtained a post as purser on one of the ships of the company to which he belonged, and he appeared at the wedding-breakfast in a suit of white ducks, a gold-laced cap, and the famous cummerbund. I have a strong suspicion that he had a revolver concealed in a mysterious pocket, from the way his hand, in moments of excitement, occasionally moved towards it, but fortunately the wedding-party was of so peaceful a description that it was not necessary to produce the weapon.

Since the exciting news of Kennie's proposed departure for Buenos Ayres, Mettie has developed nerves and hysteria. But so limited is the power of imagination or discrimination in the human mind, that I must honestly confess that I never once connected her indisposition and low spirits with the news of her cousin's departure. Mettie has added to a certain helplessness which always distinguishes her, a tendency to tears, and to sitting alone in her bedroom and sniffing dolorously; the big thin nose requires constant attention, and there are red rims round poor Mettie's eyes. The Jamiesons, who trace every variation in life to a love affair, are not long of course in coming to the right and the sentimental—nay, from the Jamieson point of view, the only reasonable explanation of this change in their little cousin. But Mettie has entreated them to say nothing, and to let her suffer in silence, and they are too loyal to betray her interesting confidences. Kennie himself is, I believe, still unaware of the interest he is exciting in Mettie's gentle breast, but doubtless the little woman's extreme timidity, and her clinging disposition, appeal in no small measure to the Defender of the Sex. Mettie raises meek, adoring eyes to the Pirate's ruddy face, under the gold-laced cap, and murmurs with clasped hands: 'You will never come back to us—I know it, I feel it! You will be murdered by some gang of cut-throats, and then what will I—I mean your mother, do?' The Pirate plumes himself and struts, and the dangers that his little cousin has so powerfully depicted for him make his young heart swell.

The village church was quite full of spectators and friends; nearly all our acquaintances in the village wore new gowns—or apparently new gowns—for the wedding. Mrs. Lovekin, in a black cloth mantle with bead trimming, showed guests into their pews, and directed the children at the doorway into giving a ringing cheer as the bride drove up to the church. It was whispered by a wag that Mrs. Lovekin would like to don a surplice and officiate at the interesting ceremony herself. There was a party in white cotton gloves, who banged doors and shouted 'Drive on!' and it was hard to realize that this was the Jamiesons' odd man and gardener, transformed for the occasion. He wore a large white ribbon rosette in his button-hole, and all the morning he had been busy erecting an archway over the gate at Belmont with Union Jacks displayed thereon, out of consideration, as he explained, to the late Captain Jamieson, he being military. The Miss Traceys were resplendent in brown dresses and profuse lace neckties, securely anchored to their chests by massive brooches, the dresses were afterwards mentioned in an account of the wedding in the local paper, and it was cut out and carefully kept by the Miss Traceys, who pasted the interesting news in a small album for news-cuttings which they bought for the purpose.

At the Jamieson's little house there was, I understand, a wild state of confusion and energy from a very early hour in the morning, and looking-glasses and hand-mirrors were in great demand. The centre of interest there, it seems, was Kate's bedroom, where the whole of The Family congregated to give Kate a last kiss before the veil was put on, and to wish her happiness again and again. George, who throughout the entire proceedings made a laudable attempt to appear calm, at last told his sister that it really was time to start, and the carriage rolled down the hill, and Kate Jamieson alighted from it, and walked up the aisle of the old church leaning upon her brother's arm. Eliza Jamieson was busy with a note-book the whole time, and almost one seemed to begin to see the wedding through her journalistic eyes.

Our curate's wife who is still far from strong, asked Palestrina to look after Peggy, who expressed a wish to see the wedding, and I was interested to find how many little games Peggy had invented for herself, by way of getting through the tedium of a service—games which I imagine she had been preparing during the many services which a curate's little girl is supposed to attend.

'If you press your eyes to the back of your head as far as you can,' she whispered to me, 'you can see green and red and blue spots, and then open them and you can see green and red and blue spots round father.' And again: 'I can say, "We beseech Thee!" seven times over while the choir are singing it, if we have Jackson's *Te Deum.'* And then: 'Do you know what Georgie and I do, when we are sent to church alone? we hide in the pew until no one thinks we are there, and then we pop up in the middle of the service and begin to say the responses. When we sit with the Sunday-school children we play at "My husband and your husband," and then we each choose in turn which husband we'll have in the congregation; you see, the first man who comes in is to be the first child's husband, and the second the second child's, that's how we manage; last Sunday I got the baker's boy.'

Mr. Swinnerton was at the wedding, somewhat inclined to be consequential, as usual; but as he devoted his whole attention to Margaret, one could not but feel that his presence was acceptable. (We are on the tip-toe of expectation to know when Mr. Swinnerton will 'come to the point.') Margaret Jamieson looked after the needs of the Higgins's relations, and attended to the wants of all the humbler of the guests.

There was still another element of interest in the marriage-party, in the person of Mr. Evans, who ran down from Hampstead for it. 'If Mr. Evans comes,' Maud said, with the characteristic fine common sense of the Jamiesons, 'I want you all to understand that it is all quite over between him and me. But what I have always thought about Mr. Evans is this—that he is the sort of man who would like The Family, and I do not see why he should not take a fancy to one of the other members of it. I am quite sure his affection for me was based upon my suitability. He often told me, for instance, that he would like a wife who had been brought up to do things for herself, and could manage on a small income and dress cheaply, and I am sure we can all do that. And after all, if that is so, one of us is as suitable as the other. He had very definite ideas about a wife; but I couldn't help feeling all the time that it was someone like ourselves that he had in his mind. He seemed to have a great dread of anyone who was too smart; and I said to him at the time—for of course we both talked about our families a good deal, as one does in the first stages—that we were all very homely sort of people. I could always put myself in the background if he seemed, for instance, to take a fancy to Gracie. And Grade herself has often said that she thinks she would like a man to wear a white watered-silk waistcoat.'

Gracie looked quite pleased with the arrangement, and Mr. Evans was asked down 'as a friend.' And I should here like to record—only of course it is going too far ahead—that before the summer was over, Mr. Evans, charmed with The Family, as Maud felt he would be, and convinced of their suitability, had chosen Gracie from amongst the remaining Miss Jamiesons who were still at the disposal of those who seek a wife. Gracie's energy charmed Mr. Evans. He often said afterwards that he believed he had got the pick of the basket after all.

It was quite evident to me, and I believe to most of the Jamiesons' guests, that one of the mysteries, so dear to the hearts of Stowel, was in preparation for the wedding afternoon. Not even my sister and I had been initiated into the secret; but Mrs. Jamie-son, it must be confessed, took away from the shock of surprise which might have been ours, by referring during the whole afternoon to the entertainment which was to take place later. The Jamiesons had decided that the lawn, newly mown, was to be suddenly cleared of trestle-tables and garden-chairs, and that a small band of musicians was to spring up unexpectedly out of the ground, as it were, and that everyone was to know suddenly that they were in the midst of an impromptu dance. Now, Mrs. Jamieson, nervously expectant, and half fearing from the detached manners of her daughters (so well did the Miss Jamiesons simulate their ignorance of what was before them) that they must indeed have forgotten about the dance, interrupted every conversation by creeping up to them in her melancholy, quiet way, and saying, 'Shall I get them to clear away now?'

'It's to be impromptu, mamma,' entreated the Miss Jamiesons, in agitated whispers. It had been decided between them that Gracie, as the youngest of the party, should exclaim suddenly, by some happy inspiration, 'I vote we dance;' and that then, in a perfectly easy and natural manner, guests and entertainers alike should, with the utmost friendliness, help to push back the tables and chairs into the lilac-bushes, and that then the musicians should be hastily summoned from the kitchen, where they were to have tea. Before that time arrived, the unfortunate Mrs. Jamieson had, as one might say, almost skimmed the cream off the whole thing. Her nervousness would not allow her to rest, and in the end, she had established the musicians in the three chairs so artlessly prepared for them under the chestnut-tree; and there they were with fiddle and concertina, long before Gracie had found an opportunity of making her impromptu suggestion. Their sudden appearance, one could not but feel, detracted from the unprepared effect that had been intended, and they stood waiting to begin with quite a forlorn appearance, until the Pirate, for whom the arrival of the hour means the arrival of the man (if the Pirate is anywhere about), called out in his loud tones, 'Strike up, you fellows, and let us have a dance!' and the very next moment, the white drill suit and the gold-laced cap of Kennie might have been seen in the middle of the lawn. He gallantly seized Mettie round the waist, and scattered the guests by the onslaught and the fierce charge he made upon them, and had soon cleared a space in which he footed it gaily. The Higgins's, who had been rather shy during the reception, hastened to find partners, and warmed to the occasion at once. Young Abel Higgins, the handsome young farmer from Dorming, said it was the pleasantest entertainment he had ever been at. 'There is no cliquism about it,' he remarked. 'You just say to a girl, "Will you dance?" and up she comes; it doesn't matter if she's a lord's daughter!'

Mr. Swinnerton devoted much of his attention and his conversation to me during the afternoon. He discussed what he calls 'military matters' at great length, pointing out the mistakes of every General in South Africa, at the same time clearly stating what Mr. Swinnerton would have done under similar circumstances, and in lamenting the inefficiency of the War Office. Later in the afternoon, however, when he found me where, as I hoped, I had effectually concealed myself behind a laurel-bush, Mr. Swinnerton plunged heavily into the question of marriage, and this, as Maud would say, was surely a very hopeful sign. I was disappointed however, to find that his views regarding the happy state of matrimony seemed to have been made almost entirely from one point of view, and that point of view himself.

'Don't you think,' he began ponderously, as he seated himself beside me after the rather heavy fatigue of dancing on a lawn to the strains of a band that did not keep scrupulous time—'don't you think that a man ought to see a girl in her own home before he makes up his mind?'

I dissented, on the plea of over-cautiousness, but Mr. Swinnerton did not hear me.

'What I think,' he went on, 'is that marriage is a serious undertaking for a man, and that one ought to be very sure of one's own mind.'

I admitted the seriousness of matrimony, but thought it applied equally to the woman.

This remark also seemed to escape Mr. Swinnerton's attention. Indeed, I found that what is extremely irritating about this fellow is that his mind never diverges from his own topic; he seems quite incapable of excursions into the thoughts and feelings of the persons he addresses, but plods steadily on his own path, pleased to give his own views, and quite unaffected by the differences of opinion that are offered him. There is a legend of my childhood that records that a man once said, 'It is bitt—' and then went to sleep for a thousand years, and when he woke up he said, '—erly cold.' I am often reminded of this story when I listen to Mr. Swinnerton's plodding conversation.

'What I feel is,' he went on—and one knew that no fatigue on the part of the listener would be noticed by him—'what I feel is, that the man being the head of the woman, he should always choose someone who is docile and good-tempered, and perhaps above all things, a good cook. That's the very first thing I would teach a woman—to be a good cook. It's so important for a man to have his meals really nice and nicely served. Don't you agree with me?'

'It is very important,' I said.

'I am so glad you agree with me.' Mr. Swinnerton occasionally remarks on an agreeable clause in one's conversation, whereas a disagreement never even penetrates his mind. 'Of course, you fellows with your mess and all that, can scarcely realize how necessary it is that a man's wife should be a thorough good cook. And then she ought to be thoroughly domesticated,' went on Mr. Swinnerton's heavy voice, 'a woman should not always be wanting to go out in the evening. What I feel is that the home should constitute the woman's happiness.'

'And cooking?' I said.

'Yes, and cooking,' said Mr. Swinnerton. 'I do not want my wife to have any money; I had much rather she had to come to me for things. I am not greedy about money. I am comfortably off, but I think a man should have entire control of the purse. One could knock off any expenditure on a wife's dress, if that is the case. Ladies like a new bonnet, and I should always give my wife a new bonnet if things had been nice.'

I remarked that Mr. Swinnerton was very generous.

'I know I am generous. Of course, a man gives up a great deal when he marries, but I do not know that in the matter of expense it would cost me more to keep a small house than to pay for lodgings.'

'It depends,' I said, 'what wages you give your wife. An occasional new bonnet would not be an extravagant salary, if she turned out to be a really good cook.'

For the first time Mr. Swinnerton seemed struck by the wisdom of my remarks. 'No, it would not,' he said—'it would not. I know that I would make a good husband,' he remarked; 'and I feel that I have a future before me in the volunteers.'

Margaret joined us at this moment, and Swinnerton smiled indulgently at her, without offering, however, to give her his seat. I do not think that Margaret noticed this, as she did not notice any omission on Mr. Swinnerton's part.

'I hope you are not very tired,' she said. 'Your journey from London and then this little dance, must be very fatiguing I am afraid.'

'Men don't get tired,' said Mr. Swinnerton grandiosely, and he looked towards me for applause. He did not, however, ask her to dance, and Margaret moved away to attend to other guests.

'She's a very nice-looking girl,' said Mr. Swinnerton approvingly, 'and a well-brought-up girl, too.'

So I suppose it is still hopeful, as the Jamiesons would say. But I pray that Margaret Jamieson will remove Mr. Swinnerton hence when she has married him.

Kate and Mr. Ward drove to the station in the best landau and pair of horses from Stowel Inn. Mr. Ward was so upset from first to last by the ceremonies and the heat, that his conical-shaped head, covered with the dew of nervous perspiration, steamed like a kettle; but his affection for his bride and his evident delight and pride in her were undeniable, and although resenting in his mild way the stinging shower of rice with which he was pelted, and the usual facetious jokes that were made on the bride and bridegroom, Mr. Ward nevertheless beamed with good-nature all the time.

Palestrina made me laugh when she came home in the evening. She had been down to the village to see the Pettifers and to show them her wedding finery, as she promised to do, for Mrs. Pettifer is ill in bed again, and was unable to stand at the church door with the rest of the crowd to see the wedding-party. My sister found the old lady weeping bitterly, and for a long time she could not guess the cause of her distress, until at last a remark of her husband's explained it. 'She do take on like that tur'ble queer,' he said, 'as soon as ever the wedding-bells ring after a marriage is over.'

'Yes,' said Mrs. Pettifer; 'I always say to myself "she's got him, and he ain't disappointed her after all."'

Kennie sailed for Buenos Ayres the day after the wedding, and Mettie walked over to see us, being sent on some errand, I have no doubt, where she would be more usefully employed than in getting in the way of the staff of workers who were clearing up after yesterday's festivities. Mettie brought over Mrs. Ward's first telegram received that morning from Dover, and said it was too funny to think of Kate being Mrs. Ward. 'Kate Ward,' she said, with one of her curious little chirruping laughs, 'Kate Ward, do look at it!' And we dutifully replied that it certainly seemed the height of drollery.

Palestrina is not perfectly just to me when Mettie comes to call. She always remembers something important which she has until this moment forgotten, and with apologies to Mettie she flies off to do it, and I am left with our caller. And then the marriage question is in full swing before one can prevent it. Mettie says she would never, **never** allow a man to know that she cared for him, and that no nice girl would. Did I think that if a girl never gave any evidence of her love and died, that it would be a very pitiful end. And of course I said that the pathos of the thing would strike one directly.

'After death,' said Mettie, 'she might still be his good angel. It is very strange,' she said, 'to think of becoming a being with wings. Do you know I often wonder what those wings can be like, and I cannot imagine them made of anything but white ostrich feathers, which I must say would look very pretty. . . . I am sure it is a brave thing to part and say nothing, but do you think that one might write?'

It was only then, at that precise moment, that I in any way connected Mettie's remarks with the thought of the Pirate Boy, now a purser in the—Line.

'My dear Mettie,' I said, 'I should certainly write to him—write often, write affectionately, send him your photograph, work him a housewife for his cabin, carve him a frame for your photograph. I am delighted—'

'Oh! but nothing is settled yet,' simpered Mettie.

It has sometimes struck me since, although one generally denies the suggestion, that the first sentiment of love-making may emanate from the woman's mind. But probably the Pirate will never know that it was not his own idea that he should fall in love with Mettie.

This evening I was looking over a lot of old letters, such as our fathers and mothers used to keep, and put away in drawers with bits of ribbon tied round them, in the days when there was more time for that sort of thing than there is now. And I came across the following letter, written in ink that has grown rather faded, and dated 1845. It describes a wedding, and I have saved it from a number of other letters which I have destroyed, to stick it into my diary as an appropriate sort of ending to my entries for today. The letter is a genuine one, and I have the original of it beside me now.

MY DEAREST AUNT,

'You wished to hear all about our doings on Thursday. Though I dare say you have heard many editions of the affairs of that day, I take the earliest opportunity of relating to you, as I promised, my version of it, though how often was it wished that dear aunt and uncle had themselves been present to illuminate the picture.

We all assembled at a quarter past ten o'clock. The married ladies (and gentlemen, whether they were in that happy state or not) remained in the drawing-room, till, at a given signal, the bride descended, followed by her bridesmaids—first Emily and myself, then Anne and Jane Schofield, then Anna and Eliza Schofield. The four first were in pink, the two last in blue. After talking over matters a little, we entered our respective carriages, mamma going in the first carriage, and papa and Mary bringing up the rear. We went through the ceremony very well. Mary responded in a perfectly clear and audible voice; but once the worthy bridegroom faltered, and as I stood next to him could perceive he was somewhat agitated. The ceremony of kissing being finished, we returned from church, when numerous and costly presents were exhibited to the eyes, and amongst them none more beautiful than my dear uncle and aunt's. But, by way of parenthesis, mamma wishes me to ask you, as Mary has two silver canisters, whether you would have any objection to change the kind and elegant expression of your feeling for Mary into a silver waiter. Knowing your kindness, we sent it by Uncle Kelsall. Now to proceed. We descended to breakfast—a most important business, which occupied us a considerable time—in the middle of which Uncle Ainsworth produced a bunch of grapes, and signified his intention of drinking Mary Schofield's health in the red juice of the grape. He immediately expressed the juice and suited the action to the word. Robert Amcliffe made a beautiful speech—quite a gem. We then proceeded to dress the bride in travelling attire. Then came the dreadful moment of parting. Mamma and papa got over it most wonderfully; suffice it to say our sisters' tears flowed most copiously on that day. After her departure, we took a drive to restore us to that harmony of spirits so desirable when persons are the entertainers of others. We drove through Hyde Park and Regent's Park in procession, and stopped to walk in the Zoological Gardens, coveting the society of the brute creation as well as the rational. We then returned to dinner, which was at seven, when, to our indescribable horror, on calling over the names of certain young ladies, we discovered their toilet was not complete when dinner was announced. After a small delay, however, the offenders appeared, and the business of dinner was commenced with astonishing vigour. There is no occasion to describe to you the manners and customs of a dinner-table, as a sameness must naturally pervade all such employments. We ladies at length signified our intention of leaving the gentlemen masters of the field, and Uncle Jesse came out with us and went to bed. We proceeded to enjoy a small quadrille, till I suppose the sound of feet called the other portion of the community from below. After tea and a little display of musical powers, we had another quadrille; but this did not occur till Emily was gone. We finally separated at half-past eleven. We have heard twice or three times from the newly-married people. They are in Bath to-day. Will you excuse, my dear aunt, this dreadful scrawl, but I have had so many notes to write, added to which I have sprained my right arm, which is now pleading to be spared any further exertions. Hoping that dear uncle and yourself, as well as dear Sarah, are well, and again begging to be excused this unconnected epistle, With united love to all, Believe me,

'Your very affectionate niece, 'MARGARET M. TAYLOR.
'MECKLENBURGH SQUARE, ' *August,* 1845.'

CHAPTER XIV

MY leg, 'my best leg,' as poor Beau Brummell used to say, has been hurting rather, for the last week or two. I do not know how Palestrina has discovered this, but the dear little woman is looking harassed and anxious, and she is trying to inveigle me into going up to London again, to get further advice from my doctor. She has broached the subject in several ways. There is a play going on at present which she would much like to see, if I will be kind enough to take her to London for a couple of days. Or there is some shopping which she wants to do, and she must have my advice on the subject. I believe that she does not like to allow, even to herself, that I ought to go expressly to see the surgeon, but she means to throw out the suggestion when we shall be in town together, and in this way she has decided, with her usual thoughtfulness, to spare me the anticipation of hearing that I am not going on as well as I ought to be doing. It is, however, much too hot to think of going up to London, so for the present none of Palestrina's deep-laid plans have been successful. It is broiling hot weather even down here in the country, but the mornings are cool and fresh, and after tossing about half the night, I generally get up and go for a feeble sort of walk before breakfast. It is extraordinary how new and fresh the world feels in the early morning, while the dew is still on the grass, and the birds are singing without any fear that their concert will be stopped or disturbed by passers-by.

On my way home this morning I passed the Jamiesons' little house, and I was hailed to come in by the flutter of nearly a dozen dinner-napkins, waved to me from the window of the breakfast-room. It is impossible to pass Belmont without being asked to come in, or to leave the hospitable little house without an invitation to stay a little longer. Monday—this was Monday—is what the Jamiesons call 'one of our busiest mornings,' and I think that our good friends talk almost more than usual on the days on which they are most engaged.

As I entered the room, two of The Family had already finished their breakfast, and were busy at a side-table, driving their sewing-machines. The whirring noise, added to the amount of talking that was going on, had rather a bewildering effect at first. There was, besides, the added confusion attendant upon what is known as 'getting George off.' The process seems to consist of shaking George into his City coat, brushing it, patting him on the back, telling him how nice he looks, hoping he will get down in the middle of the week, or at least not later than Friday afternoon, and giving him messages and remembrances to quite half a dozen friends in London. The Family chorus as I entered was something like this:

'Cream or sugar, weak or strong?'

'Mettie, did you get your letters?'

'Eliza, which is your napkin-ring?'

'Please say what you will have, I have asked you at least half a dozen times.'

'Do you mind the window open?'

'Does anyone hear the bus?'

'Toast or rolls?'

'Which is your napkin-ring?'

'Did anyone hear the rain last night?'

'You haven't said yet if you will have an egg.'

'Mother is not well, and is not coming down this morning.'

'Does anyone mind if we go on with our machines?'

Over and above this, snatches of newspaper were read, and numerous directions were given to a very young servant as to how things should be placed upon the table—a proceeding which usually goes on at everyone of the Jamiesons' meals.

It is known as 'training one of our village girls.'

Gracie and Eliza were the two who sat at the side-table before their whirring sewing-machines, their very spectacles nearly darting from their heads with energy and speed. George said, 'I wish one of you girls would mend my glove before I start;' and Gracie said, 'Give it to me, I can spare five minutes off lunch-time to get this finished.'

Margaret remarked, 'Mamma seems very much out of spirits to-day, and I think one of us ought to go and play draughts with her.'

Eliza took out her watch. 'I can play draughts for thirty-five minutes,' she remarked—'from eleven-five to eleven-forty—and then Gracie must take my place, as Margaret will be baking, and I have the soup-kitchen accounts to make up.'

'I did not anticipate draughts this morning,' said poor Gracie. 'I must just get this done when I go to bed.' This is the last refuge of the overdriven, and one which is so frequently alluded to by the Jamiesons, that I often fear they deny themselves the proper amount of sleep.

George here kissed each of his sisters in turn, and ran upstairs to say good-bye to his mother, while the omnibus waited at the gate.

Maud, who was trimming hats for the whole family, and who was surrounded by a curious medley of ribbons and finery, said: 'What about the Church Council work? I am afraid we have forgotten it.'

'That's my business,' said Gracie tragically; 'and I must give this up;' and she stopped her sewing-machine, and rolled the purple cotton pinafore into a tight ball and placed it on the table.

'Dear Gracie,' said Margaret, 'could I not do it? I could get it in between the Kaffirs and my baking.'

'I would offer to do it,' said Eliza, with that affectionate helpfulness which distinguishes The Family, 'only I am so filled up with soup.' Eliza referred to her soup-kitchen accounts.

The small servant here appeared at the door, and said that an old woman wanted to see Miss Grade.

'My time! my time I' said Gracie, and went to the back-door to give the last shilling of her quarter's dress-allowance to the poor woman in distress.

'The worst of playing draughts is,' said Eliza, 'that one can do nothing else at the same time, except it be to add up accounts in one's head. Otherwise I should have been only too glad. I tell you what I can do, though—I can play instead of Gracie this morning, if she won't mind my keeping the candle alight to do my Browning article after I have gone to bed.'

Mettie always offers to help everyone, but so slow is the little woman's way of working, that the energetic family of Jamieson are quite aware that probably the business will be weeks in doing, so their answers to Mettie's offers, given in a kindly voice, are always: 'My dear, you have got your letters to write, and your practising—we could not do without your singing in the evening, you know.'

Mr. Evans, who was a guest in the house for a few days, was smoking his pipe in a leisurely way in the garden, and Gracie said: 'I really do feel that I ought to give more attention to Mr. Evans, if only I had the time for it. Could one of you run into the garden and make a few pleasant remarks to him until I am ready? And this Eliza did, first glancing at her watch in the characteristic Jamieson fashion, and coming in presently to say that she had sat 'for ten solid minutes doing nothing, and that she does wish men had more resources of their own.'

It would have been useless to suggest that the work should stop for a whole summer day. A child came in with some flowers as an offering to the Miss Jamiesons, and Eliza said: 'Would you mind putting them down somewhere, my dear? I will try to get a minute to arrange them by-and-by.' And then the machines began again, and I walked on homewards, and enjoyed a long, hot morning in the garden with a book.

The garden was very shady and pleasant, and one thought regretfully of the Jamiesons sitting indoors with their sewing-machines. Palestrina came out presently in a gray dress, very soft and cool-looking, and with a big sunshade over her head. She sat down beside me, and said in an off-hand way and a determination to be congratulatory, which was very suspicious: 'I have got a pressing invitation for you.' And she handed me a letter from Kate Ward.

Mrs. Ward wrote upon the almost immaculate notepaper which is affected by brides. I have often noticed that this superfine quality of paper is one of the first extravagances of young married life, as it is one of the first economies of a later date, and a little judgment will soon show how long a woman has been married by merely looking at her notepaper. Cream-laid, with a gold address at the top, bespeaks the early days of matrimony, and a descent through white stamping, no stamping, Hieratica to Silurian note, marks the different stages of the rolling years.

Kate said (on the best Court note) that she would never forgive us if we did not come and see her in her new home. James had been generous in the extreme, and they had bought everything 'plain but good' for the house. And the whole expense of it had been covered by exactly the sum of money that they had laid by for the purpose. Kate continued: 'But I will not bore you with a description of the house, for I want you to see it for yourselves,' and then entered upon the usual Jamieson descriptive catalogue of every piece of furniture and every wall-paper which she had purchased.

I handed the letter back to Palestrina, who was sitting in an exaggerated attitude of ease and indifference on the edge of my deck-chair, and said to her, 'Why leave Paradise? London will be atrocious in this hot weather, and I believe it would be tempting Providence to quit this garden.'

'I am afraid it will give great disappointment to Kate if we do not go,' said Palestrina, in a tone of voice which suggested that she had been prepared for opposition, and had rehearsed her own arguments beforehand. 'After all, she lives in the suburbs, and has a garden of her own, and we need not stay more than two or three days.'

'We shall have to do so much admiring,' I said, smothering a yawn. 'I know what brides are! You, Palestrina, probably know exactly the right thing to say about newly-laid linoleum and furniture which is plain but good. But I never do.'

'I think I should like to go,' said Palestrina, putting the matter upon personal grounds, as I knew she would do when she had entirely made up her mind that I must go up to London. What pressure she had brought to bear upon Mrs. Ward to induce her to invite us to the new house I cannot say, but some instinct told me that Kate had been warned to write a letter which might be handed to me to read.

I pointed out to Palestrina that, much as I should miss her at home, I should not stand in the way of her paying a visit to her old friend.

'I have accepted for us both from Thursday to Tuesday,' said Palestrina firmly. 'Oh, by-the-by,' she said, rising and going indoors, 'I just sent a line to Dr. Fergus at the same time to say that you will look in and see him one morning, just to see that you are going on all right.'

'You also were up early?' I said to the diplomat who smiled at me from under her big umbrella without a vestige of shame at her own cunning. 'I don't think it is fair on a crippled man to get up early and send off letters by the early post. It's a mean trick.'

'You were up half the night,' said Palestrina, nodding her head at me, 'for I heard you.' And she crossed the lawn and went indoors again.

The following Thursday we took train for Clark-ham. I had never stayed in this part of the world before, till we came to visit Kate, and the suburb where she lives seems to me to be rather a pleasant place, with broad roads, over whose walls and palings, shrubs and red maples and other trees hang invitingly. And it is so near London, that a very short run in the train takes one to Victoria Station. But the neighbourhood is not fashionable, and I cannot help remarking the apologetic tone with which everyone we meet, speaks of living here.

The Wards' house is a very nice little place, with very new wall-papers and very clean curtains and slippery floors, upon which art rugs slide dangerously. There is a small garden with a lawn and a brown hawthorn tree upon it, and there are two trim little maids who wait upon one excellently well. Kate is a thorough good manager, and her whole household reminds one of those pages on household management which one sees in magazines, describing the perfect equipment of a house—its management and the rules to be observed by a young housekeeper.

There is a place for everything, and Kate says her wedding-presents are a great assistance in giving a home-like look to the house.

Mr. Ward leaves home at half-past nine every morning, and Kate shakes him into his coat in exactly the same way George used to be shaken into his, and stands at the hall-door with a bright smile on her face, until James has got into the morning bus and driven away, in a manner that is very wifely and commendable.

The unpretentious little household seems to be a very happy one, and Kate was quite satisfied with the praise which Palestrina bestowed upon everything.

'Of course,' she said, 'the great drawback is that the place is so unfashionable;' and we warmly protested against that mattering in the very least. But Kate said, with her usual common sense: 'It does matter, really. No one thinks anything of you if you live here, and nearly everyone who has enough money always leaves directly. Still'—cheerfully—'one must expect some drawbacks, and I do think I have been very lucky. James is goodness itself, and quite a number of people have been to call.'

We found to our dismay that Kate had, with the laudable intention of amusing us, accepted several invitations to what are called 'the last of the summer gaieties.' There were tea-parties and garden-parties given by her friends, to which we were expected to go, and her very nearest neighbours, who are generally known as the 'Next Doors,' actually invited us to dine.

'This afternoon' Kate said, 'is the day of the Finlaysons' garden-party. They are frightfully rich people—ironmongers in the City; but you never saw such greenhouses and gardens as they have got! Do put on your best dress,' she said to Palestrina, 'and look nice; people here seem to dress so smartly for this sort of thing,'

I think, indeed, it was the very grandest party to which I have ever had an invitation. Everyone seemed to sail about in a most regal fashion, in gowns of some rich stuff, and there was such an air of magnificence about the whole thing, that one hardly dared to speak above a whisper. There was a marquee on the lawn, with most expensive refreshments inside, and a great many waiters handing about things on trays. Mrs. Finlayson spoke habitually—at least at parties—in an exalted tone of voice, which one wondered if she used when, for instance, she was adding up accounts or saying her prayers. It was difficult to imagine that the voice could have been intended for private use—it was such a very public, almost a platform voice, and the accent was most finished and aristocratic.

The Miss Finlaysons, in exquisite blue dresses and very thin shoes, also sailed about and shook hands with their guests, in a cold proud way which was very effective. Young Finlayson was frankly supercilious and condescending; and there was a schoolboy in a tall hat, who was always alluded to as 'our brother at Eton.' The excellent old papa of the firm of Finlayson and Merritt was really the most human and the least alarming of the whole party. He seemed quite pleased when Palestrina, in her soft gurgling way, admired his greenhouses and peaches, and he led her back to where his lady ('wife' is too homely a term) was standing in a throne-room attitude on the lawn, and remarked genially: 'This young lady has just been admiring our little place, Lavinia.'

'Indeed,' said my sister, 'it seems to me very charming, and—'

'Hush, hush!' said Mrs. Finlayson playfully, but with an undercurrent of annoyance in her party voice; 'I won't hear a word said in its praise—it is just a step to the West End.'

'What is the actual distance,' I began.

It was old Finlayson who rescued me from my dilemma, and explained that until five years ago they had had a very tidy little 'ouse at 'ampstead, and that this present location, although so magnificent, was, in the eyes of his lady, really a stepping-stone to further grandeur and a more fashionable locality.

The Next Doors were introduced to us at this party, and we were much struck by the fact that, although they seemed appropriately lodged in a place well suited to them, and in a society certainly not inferior to themselves, they, too, instantly began to apologize for living at Clarkham.

'One feels so lost in a place like this,' said Mrs. Next Door, 'and although the boys are so happy with their tennis and things on Saturday afternoons, I cannot help feeling that it is a great drawback to the girls to live here.'

A band began to play under the trees, and Palestrina said to me, with one of her low laughs: 'I wonder if I shall begin to sail about soon? Isn't it funny! They all do it, and now that the band has begun I feel that I must do it too.'

The Miss Finlaysons came up at intervals and introduced young men to her, in a spasmodic sort of way. When one least expected it, someone in a tall hat and a long frock-coat was placed before Palestrina, and a Miss Finlayson said, quite sharply: 'May I introduce—Mr. Smith—'and then as suddenly retired. There was nothing for it but to make a little tepid conversation to the various Mr. Smiths, and Sonnenscheins, and Seligmanns who were in this way presented, and we noticed that almost every one of them began his conversation by saying, 'Been going out a great deal lately? Done the Academy?' And then moved off to be introduced to someone else.

The young men were very supercilious and grand, and we could only account for it, on discussing the matter afterwards, by supposing that they thought Palestrina was a Clarkham young lady, and that this was their way of showing their superiority to her, One or two had certainly said to us with a dubious air, 'Do you live in the Pork?' But it was not until the quieter moments that followed the stress of this regal party, that we at all realized that this meant, did we live in Clarkham Park.

Kate Ward was very agreeable and pleasant to every one, and was voted a nobody directly, and we heard it remarked that she had 'no style.' I think Kate must have overheard the remark, for she became a little nervous towards the end of the afternoon, and presently said: 'Perhaps we ought to be going?' But young Finlayson was here suddenly introduced to her by one of his sisters, and Kate thought it necessary to make a few remarks before saying good-bye. She said something pretty about his sisters, who are undoubtedly handsome girls, and Mr. Finlayson said bitterly: 'Yes, a good many so-called beauties in London would have to shut up shop if my sisters appeared in the Row. It is a beastly shame they have got to live down here!'

Kate said: 'But I suppose they go to town occasionally?'

'Yes,' said Mr. Finlayson;' but they ought to have their Park hacks, and do things in style. It is a shame the governor does not take a house in the West End.'

My sister tried to look sympathetic.

'However,' said Mr. Finlayson more hopefully, 'we have taken a bit of a shoot in Scotland this year, so I hope the girls will have some society. Well, it is a deer forest really, and a very fine house and grounds,' amended Mr. Finlayson, with a burst of candour.

Mrs. Finlayson sailed up, and stooped to make a few remarks about the gaiety of the past season to us. She said that she and her daughters were in demand everywhere, and that the other night in a West End theatre every lorgnette in the house was turned towards their box. 'Rupert, of course, has his own chambers in St. James's, and knows everyone.'

The Miss Finlaysons shook hands, and said goodbye with their usual lofty condescension, and each said, 'Going on anywhere?' to which we could only reply humbly that we had no further engagements for that afternoon.

Kate praised the party all the way home, and then said, with a burst of feeling: 'Oh, how I do wish I were a swell! I know it's wicked, but I would snub one or two people.'

The next morning, being Sunday, we went to church, and the feeling of equality with the rest of mankind which this gives one was very refreshing after the magnificence and social distinctions about which we had been learning so much during the last few days. But even in church one may notice how superior some families in Clarkham are to others. The pew-letting of the church seems to have been conducted on principles other than those recommended in Holy Writ. Richer folk, those with gold chains, for whom we learn precedence should not be accorded, occupied the front pews, furnished with red cushions and Prayer-Books with silver corners, while the humbler sort were accommodated with seats under the gallery. The Finlaysons sailed in rather late, with a rustle of their smart dresses, and kneeled to pray on very high hassocks, their elbows just touching the book-board in front of them, their faces inadequately covered with their tightly-gloved hands. The Next Doors had a pew half-way up the middle aisle. The day was hot, and the clergyman, a small devout-looking man, very earnest and really eloquent, was guilty some-times in moments of excitement of dropping aitches. This of course may have been the result of the hot weather. It was something of a shock to notice, that the little Next Doors—terrible children, of high spirits and pugnacious dispositions—were allowed to giggle unreproved at each omission of the aspirate on the part of the preacher. The Next Doors overtook us on our way out of church, and two of the pugnacious children, having dug each other with their elbows, and fought round me for permission to walk home with me and talk about the war, threw light upon their behaviour in church by remarking with smiling self-satisfaction, 'Papa says we ought always to giggle when Mr. Elliot drops his aitches, to show that we know better. . . .' Little brutes!

We spent a lazy afternoon under the brown hawthorn tree on the little lawn, and Thomas drove down to see Palestrina, and good Kate Ward put forth her very best efforts to give us a sumptuous cold supper. We found, to our surprise, that nightingales sing down here, and we sat on the lawn till quite late listening to them. Mr. and Mrs. Ward slipped their hands into one another's in the dark, and appeared to be most happy and contented.

'I am glad we came,' said Palestrina, that night when Mrs. Ward had quitted the room. 'Dear old Kate!'

CHAPTER XV

ON Monday I went to see Dr. Fergus about my leg, and did not get a very good report of it.

We returned from Clarkham on one of the hottest days I ever remember, and found Mrs. Fielden waiting for us in the hall.

'Everyone seems to have come over to hear about your London visit,' said Mrs. Fielden lightly, 'for I found Mr. Ellicomb and Maud Jamieson here when I came in.'

She began pouring out tea for us both as she spoke, and she signalled something to Palestrina, who replied as she stooped down to cut some cake: 'Another operation—yes, four or five weeks in bed at least.'

'I sent Maud and Mr. Ellicomb home together,' said Mrs. Fielden, smiling. 'He, poor man, is in a great state of mental perturbation, for it seems that he has heard that in South Africa pigs are fed upon arum lilies, and that so delicate is the flesh of the pork thus produced that some flower-growers in the Channel Isles are cultivating arum lilies for the purpose of feeding pigs, and to produce the same delicious pork. He was so agitated that he got up from his chair and walked up and down the room, repeating over and over again, "Arum-fed pork! Monstrous, monstrous!" I really did not know how to comfort him, so I sent him home with Maud Jamieson which seemed to please him very much.'

'And you,' I said, 'following the Jamieson train of thought, have been saying to yourself ever since, "Is there anything in it?"'

'She certainly had a soothing effect upon him,' said Mrs. Fielden.

'Then,' said I, 'the second stage has been reached. When all the Jamiesons are married, I think I shall feel that romance is over.'

'I know they have been to tea at the farm,' said Mrs. Fielden, 'because Mr. Ellicomb talked so much about his blue china, and Maud said a woman's hand was needed in the house.'

'I wonder,' I said, 'what will be the special objection that Maud will raise when she becomes engaged to Mr. Ellicomb? He is not called Albert; he does not wear a white watered-silk waistcoat; his hair is certainly his own; and his mother is dead, so it cannot be said that he too closely resembles her.'

One of the objections raised by Maud to a candidate for her hand, was that he was far too like his mother—a really delightful woman—but Maud declared, with tears, that she could never really look up to a man who was so like his mamma.

'At present,' said Mrs. Fielden, 'the blue china seems to be all in his favour; but one cannot feel sure that it will not be an obstacle later on, or Mr. Ellicomb's High Church principles, perhaps, may prove a deterrent to her ideas of perfect happiness.'

'I wish,' said Palestrina, 'that Margaret's affairs were more settled. This summer has been a trying one for her.'

'Oh, I forgot to tell you,' said Mrs. Fielden, 'that that was one of Maud's reasons for coming over to see you. She told me that Mr. Swinnerton is coming to pay them a visit. He has written, it seems, to make the offer himself, and Maud says she thinks it will be all right now.'

Mrs. Fielden was in one of her most light-hearted moods. After the heat of the day there came a delightful coolness, and she stayed chatting till nearly dinner-time, and then decided that she would remain to dinner if we asked her.

'I have three dear old sisters-in-law staying with me, said Mrs. Fielden, 'and they will doubtless drag all the ponds for my body.'

'Won't they be anxious about you?' asked Palestrina.

'Perhaps,' said Mrs. Fielden, raising her pretty eyebrows in the old affected way; 'but then they will appreciate me so much more when I come back to them from the grave.'

We sat out on the lawn after dinner till it was quite dark, and only Mrs. Fielden's white dress was visible in the gloom. For some reason best known to herself, she put off her wilful mood out there in the gloom of the garden. She was not regal, not even amusing, only charming and full of a lovely kindness. Half the conversation between her and Palestrina began with the words, 'Do you remember?' as they recalled old jokes and stories. Then her ever-present gaiety broke out again, and she laughed and said: 'I believe I am becoming reminiscent. Why doesn't someone sit upon me, or tell me they will order the carriage for me if I really must go? But it is heavenly here in the cool;—and in heaven, you know, we shall probably all be reminiscent.'

Ten o'clock struck from the tower of the church down below in the village, and Mrs. Fielden said that now she really must go, or she would find the sisters-in-law saying a Requiem Mass for her, and Palestrina went indoors to order the carriage.

'To-morrow,' I said, 'I am going to have my last dissipation. I am going to the Traceys' tea-party.'

'I am certainly going too,' said Mrs. Fielden. 'I believe I am getting as gay as the Miss Traceys themselves, though I can't help remarking that no one who goes to these tea-parties ever seems to be amused when they get there.'

'Judging from my own standard of what I find amusing,' I said, 'I should be inclined to say that Stowel never enjoys itself extravagantly. Our neighbours never refuse invitations to even the smallest party; but the pleasure that they get from them, if it exists at all, is carefully concealed.'

'I have felt that myself,' said Mrs. Fielden. 'I really don't begin to enjoy them till I get home.'

'I believe you always enjoy yourself,' I said resentfully.

After a little time Mrs. Fielden said wistfully, 'You don't think there is only a certain amount of happiness in the world, do you, Hugo? And that if one person gets a great deal, it means that another will get less?'

She asks one questions in this way sometimes, as though one were a superior being who could dispel her perplexities for her.

'Probably,' I said, 'you know ten thousand times more about the subject than I do. You are happy, and I philosophize about it. Tell me which of us is most fitted to give a lecture on the subject?'

I thought Mrs. Fielden was going to say something after that, for she stretched out her hand in a certain impulsive way she has got, and gave mine just one moment's friendly pressure in the dark. And then Palestrina came back to say the carriage was at the door, and Mrs. Fielden said 'Goodnight.'

I remember two things about the Miss Traceys' party—first, that Mrs. Fielden was not there, for one of the old sisters-in-law was ill suddenly, and she could not leave her; and the other thing I remember about it is that it was the last occasion on which I ever saw Margaret Jamieson look pretty.

There have been some strange innovations in tea-parties ever since Mrs. Taylor gave hers to meet The Uncle, and sent out visiting-cards instead of notes. Instead of having tea in the dining-room, all sitting round the table, as used to be the custom; it seems that dressing-tables are often brought down from upstairs and extended across the window. These are covered with white tablecloths, and behind them two maids stand and wait. The dressing-tables are called the 'buffet,' and both tea and coffee are provided, suggesting the elegance and savour of London refreshments. This is distinctly pleasing, though it is felt that a single cup of tea drunk while standing, has not got the comfort of former old-fashioned days. Miss Belinda lives on at the little cottage with the green gate; and through the kindness of the General a lady has been found to wait upon her, and take her out to these small gaieties which she loves, and she sits shaking her poor, weak head, and muttering, 'Glory, glory, glory!' It does not occur to her to stay at home during her period of mourning, and it is acknowledged on all sides that she does not miss Lydia much. The General has not come to stay with the Taylors again. In a long letter which he wrote to me after he left, he said he would probably never come back to the place, and at the same time he thanked me in courteous, old-fashioned phraseology for being with him through what he called 'one of the dark days that come sometimes.' He would never see Miss Belinda, in spite of the many kind things he did for her; and I always feel that he resented the poor creature's long illness and weak, silly ways—which was only natural, no doubt.

The Vicar was present at his sisters' tea-party, 'although,' as Miss Ruby explained to me, 'it is not as though this were an evening entertainment. My sister and I often give these little routs without him. Still, a gentleman is always something of an ornament at a party.'

There were seven Jamiesons present, and two of them, Margaret and Maud, offered, in their usual friendly way, to walk home with Palestrina and me, Maud, one feels sure, engaged Palestrina in confidences directly; and Margaret whispered in a shy way to me, 'Do you mind coming round by the post-office? I am expecting a letter.' So we walked round by the High Street, and Margaret told me that Tudor had had to give up his visit to them, but that he was writing.

So we went into the post-office, and Margaret got her letter handed to her across the counter by the post-mistress, upon whom she bestowed a radiant smile. When we got outside she opened it and read it without a word; and then, quite suddenly, she gave a cry as though someone had struck her, and she handed the letter to me, and said: 'Oh, Hugo, read it!' And I read:

'I am sure you will be surprised when I tell you that I am going to be married; it will explain to you why it was that I was unable to fulfil my promise to come to see you. But sudden though my engagement to Miss Lloyd has been—very sudden, much more sudden indeed than I ever felt that such a serious step as marriage would be undertaken by me—I cannot but feel that it is for my happiness. Some day I hope you will make Miss Lloyd's acquaintance; she is staying with my mother just now, and she is already a great favourite. I cannot but feel that having seen so much of you and of your family last summer, and during your

stay in London, that I may have raised expectations which I find myself unable to fulfil; but I am quite sure that a man's first duty is to himself in these matters, and that he should not undertake matrimony until he is thoroughly convinced it is for his happiness. Had I not met Miss Lloyd, I may say that my intentions to you were of the most serious; and I know that I have the power in me to make any girl happy. We shall live with my mother for the first year, and then I hope to settle somewhere near London, where it will be nice for me to get into the fresh air after my work in the City.

'Yours very truly, 'TUDOR SWINNERTON.

'P.S.—Miss Lloyd and I are to be married next month in St. Luke's Church, quite near here.'

I handed the letter back to Margaret, and we never spoke the whole way home. And that was the last day I ever saw Margaret Jamieson look pretty.

CHAPTER XVI

AFTER the operation on my leg, I was laid up for a long time, and when I got about again, Palestrina and Thomas were married. Thomas has lately come into his kingdom in the shape of a lordly castle in Scotland, and for the life of me I can't say whether or not Palestrina hastened her wedding because the doctor ordered me to the North. If it were so, my sister's plans were frustrated by the fact that Thomas's ancient Scottish seat was pronounced uninhabitable by a sanitary surveyor, just as we proposed entering it under garlanded archways and mottoes on red cotton. Our old friend Mrs. Macdonald, hearing of our dilemma, very kindly invited us to stay with her while Palestrina and Thomas looked about for some little house that would take us in till their own place should be ready. The finding of the little house occupied some days, owing to the powers of imagination displayed by people when describing their property. One lady, to whom Palestrina wrote to ask if her house were to be let, replied, 'Yes, madam; this dear, delightful, pretty house is to let;' and she pointed out in a letter, some four pages long, all the advantages that would accrue to us if we took it, ending up with the suggestion, subtly conveyed, that by taking the house we should be turning her into the street, but that she would bear this indignity in consideration of receiving ten guineas a week.

Palestrina went to see it, and returned in the evening, almost in tears, to say that the house was a semi-detached villa, and that she found the week's washing spread out on the front lawn.

Thomas said that the railway companies ought to pay a percentage on all misleading advertisements which induce people to make these useless journeys.

The following day they returned from another fruitless expedition, having been to see a very small house owned by the widow of a sea-captain, with a strong Scotch accent. I have often noticed that the sea-faring man's one idea of well-invested capital is house property—perhaps he alone knows how precarious is the life of the sea. And I shall like to meet the sailor who has invested his money in a shipping concern. The widow's house was so vary small that it was almost impossible to believe that it contained the ten bedrooms as advertised in my sister's well-worn house-list. So small indeed were the rooms, that Palestrina said she felt sure that they must have been originally intended for cupboards. Nevertheless, the rent of the house was very high, and my sister ventured gently to hint this to the lady of the house—the sea-captain's widow with the strong Scotch accent.

'Of course, it is a very nice house,' she said politely; 'but the rent is a little more than we thought of paying for a house of this size.'

'I ken it's mair than the hoose is worth,' said the old dame; 'but, ye see, I'm that fond o' money—aye, I'm fearfu' fond o' money.'

Palestrina and Thomas spent most of their days in their search for a suitable house, and Mrs. Macdonald spends the greater part of her life housekeeping, so I was rather bored. What it actually is that occupies my hostess during the hours she spends in the back regions of her house, I have never been able to discover. But the fact remains that we have to get up unusually early in the morning to allow time for Mrs. Macdonald's absorbing occupation. An old-fashioned Scotswoman of my acquaintance used to refuse all invitations to leave the house on Thursdays, because, as she explained, 'I keep Thursdays for my creestal and my napery.' The rest of her week, however, was comparatively free. At Mrs. Macdonald's, house-keeping is never over. And so systematic are the rules and regulations of the house, so many and so various are the lady's keys, that one finds one's self wondering if the rules of a prison or a workhouse can be more strict, The *Times* newspaper arrives every evening after dinner; by lunch-time next day it is locked away in a cabinet, so that if one has not read the news by one o'clock, one must ask Mrs. Macdonald to let one have the keys; this she does quite good-naturedly, but I have never discovered why old newspapers should be kept with so much care. On Saturdays, an old man from the village comes in to do a little extra tidying up in the garden. At nine o'clock precisely, Mrs. Macdonald is on the doorstep of her house, with a cup of tea in her hand, and a brisk kindly greeting for John, and she stands over the old man while he drinks his tea, and then returns with the empty cup to the house.

Tuesday is the day on which her drawing-room is cleaned. At half-past nine precisely on Monday evenings Mrs. Macdonald says—'Monday, you know, is our early closing night;' and she fetches you a candle and despatches you to bed. Mrs. Macdonald and her housemaid—there seem to be plenty of servants to do the work of the house—walk the whole of the drawing-room furniture into the hall, Mrs. Macdonald loops up the curtains herself, and covers some appalling pictures and the mantelpiece-ornaments with dust-sheets. At ten o'clock she removes a pair of housemaid's gloves, and an apron which she has donned for the occasion, and says: There! that's all ready for Tuesday's cleaning;' and she briskly bids her housemaid goodnight.

On Tuesdays we are not allowed to enter the drawing-room all day, and on Wednesdays the same restrictions are placed upon the dining-room. Indeed, on no day in the week is the whole of the house available, and upon no morning of the week has Mrs. Macdonald a spare moment to herself. After breakfast, when Palestrina and Thomas have gone, she conducts me to the morning-room, and placing the *Scotsman* (the *Scotsman* is used for lighting the fires, and is formally handed to the house-maid at six o'clock in the evening) by my chair, she says, 'I hope you will be all right,' and shuts the door upon me. During the morning she pops her head in from time to time, like an attentive guard who has been told to look after a lady on a journey, and nodding briskly from the door, she asks, 'Are you all right? Sure you would not like milk or anything?' and then disappears again. With a little stretch of imagination one can almost believe that the green flag has been raised to the engine-driver, and that the train is moving off. At lunch-time she is so busy giving directions to her servants that she hardly ever hears what one says, and the most interesting piece of news is met with the somewhat irrelevant reply, 'The bread-sauce, please, Jane, and then the cauliflower.' Turning to one, she explains, 'I always train my servants myself. . . . What were you saying just now?'

'I saw in the newspaper this morning,' I repeat, that H.M.S.—has foundered with all hands.'

'In the middle of the table, if you please,' says Mrs. Macdonald; 'and then the coffee with the crystallized sugar—not the brown—and open the drawing-room windows when you have finished tidying there. . . . What were you saying? How sad these things are!'

The house is charmingly situated, with a most beautiful view over river and hills; but I really think my preoccupied friend hardly ever has time to look out of the window, and that to her, the interior of a store cupboard with neatly-filled shelves is more beautiful than anything which the realms of Nature can offer.

When Palestrina is present, Mrs. Macdonald gives her recipes for making puddings and for taking stains out of carpets, and she advises her about spring cleanings and the proper sifting of ashes at the back-door. Mrs. Macdonald was brought up in the old days, when a young lady's training and education were frankly admitted to be a training for her as a wife. She belonged to the period when a girl with a taste for music was encouraged to practise 'so that some day you may be able to play to your husband in the evenings, my dear,' and was advised to be an early riser so that the house might be comfortable and in order when her husband should descend to breakfast. And now that that husband having been duly administered to is dead, Mrs. Macdonald's homely talents, once the means to an end, have resolved themselves into an end, a finality of effort. Mrs. Macdonald was brought up to be a housekeeper, and she remains a housekeeper, and jam-pots and preserving-pans form the boundary line of her life and the limit of her horizon.

Eliza Jamieson would probably tell us that even though Mrs. Macdonald's soups and preserves are excellent, these culinary efforts should not be the highest things required of a wife by her husband, and that therefore they are not a wife's highest duty, even during the time that her husband remains with her. And she would probably point out that servants and weekly bills, and an endeavour to render this creature complacent, have ruined many a woman's life. And I laugh as I think of Palestrina's rejoinder: 'But then it is so much pleasanter when they are complacent.'

One certainly imagined that the late Mr. Macdonald must have been well looked after during his life, and it was something of a shock to me to hear the account of his death, from the lodge-keeper's wife, one afternoon when she had come in to help with the cleaning, and was arranging my dressing-table for me. The rest of my bedroom furniture was then standing in the passage, and I had found my cap in one of the spare bedrooms, and all the boots of the house in the hall.

'He was a rale decent gentleman,' said Mrs. Gemmil, 'and awfy patient with the cleaning. But I am sure, whiles I was sorry for him. He was shuftit and shuftit, and never knew in the morn whichna bed in the hoose he would be sleeping in at nicht. And we a' ken that it was the spring cleaning, when he was pit to sleep ower the stables, that was, under Providence, the death o' him. He had aye to cross ower in the wat at nicht time, and he juist took a pair o' cauld feet, and they settled on his lungs.'

The day following my chat with Mrs. Gemmil was the day Palestrina found a house such as she had been looking for all along. The day was Saturday. Overnight she had announced her intention of being away all day, and Mrs. Macdonald had said delightedly that that would suit her admirably. 'I do like the servants to have the entire day for the passages on Saturday,' she remarked.

Even when the day dawned wet and cloudy, Palestrina had not the courage to suggest that she should stay at home, and thereby interfere with the cleaning of the passages.

The house she had found seemed to be everything that was desirable, and Palestrina returned in an elated frame of mind. 'It is far away from everything,' she said, 'except the village people and the minister, and the "big hoose," as they call it, which some English bodies have rented for the autumn.'

'It can't be far from the Melfords,' said Thomas, pulling out a map. 'Yes, I thought so; they are just the other side of the loch.'

'We "mussed the connaketion "on our way back,' said Palestrina; 'and I do believe there's nothing a Scotch porter enjoys telling one so much as this.'

'I hope I am not unduly disparaging the railway system of my native land, said Thomas, 'when I say that if you go by steamer and by train it is the remark that usually greets one, and it is always made in a tone of humorous satisfaction.' And Thomas, with an exaggerated Scotch accent, which he does uncommonly well, began to tell me of their adventures. 'We had a rush for the train,' he said, 'and I told an elderly Scot, who couldn't have hurried if he had a mad bull behind him, to run and get us two first-class tickets. He walked slowly down the platform, muttering, "Furrst, furrst," and then he opened the door of a third-class carriage and shoved us in, saying, "Ye've no occasion to travel furrst when there's plenty of room in the thurrds." '

CHAPTER XVII

To get to the house, one takes a steamer to the head of the loch, and from there old Hughie drives one in the coach, and deposits one at the cross-roads where the turf, short and green, is cut into the shape of a heart. On this green heart, in the old days, the girls and men of the glen were married. They stood side by side on the upper part of the heart, which is indented, and the minister stood at the point and wedded the pair. Here one leaves the coach, and a 'machine' must take one on to the little house. A red creeper grows up its white walls, and from the terrace in front of the house, one looks down upon the little Presbyterian church and the village, and these in their turn look on to the loch and the hills on the other side.

The people in the village afford one a good deal of amusement, but we have observed that the conversation is always of theology or of the Royal Family. There is one story of the late Queen and the crown of Scotland which I have heard repeated many times with the utmost gravity in the Highlands.

'A gran' wumman' say the old villagers, 'but we were no gaein' tae gie her the croon o' Scotland. Na, na. She would hae liked fine tae hev gotten it, but we were no gaein' tae gie her the croon o' Scotland. Ye'll mind when she went tae Scotland, it was the foremost thing that she spiered tae see. And when they showed it tae her, "I would like fine tae pit it on ma heid," said she. But they said " *No.* " And syne she says, "Wad ye no let me haud it in ma haund?" But they say " *No.* " "Weel," she

says, "juist haud it aboon ma heid, and let me staun' underneath it." But they said
" *No.* " '

The villagers formed our only society until Evan Sinclair's tenants, who were
known as 'the folk at the big hoose,' came to call upon us. It was very difficult indeed, and for some time we could hardly believe that these were the Finlaysons
whom we had met at Clarkham, and who, we now remembered, had told us that
they were going to take a place in Scotland. The change in the Finlaysons is startling
and complete. It has taken them exactly two months to become Highlanders, and it
is not too much to affirm that now the whole family may be said to reek of tartan.
Only Mrs. Finlayson is unaffected by her life in the Highlands, although she says
that she knows it is fashionable to be Scottish. 'And so written up as it is at present,'
she adds; 'and all the best people taking the deer-moors. Papa and the girls think all
the world of Scotland. But no one can say it is comfortable, I'm sure.'

The Finlaysons have a piper, and young Mr. Finlayson wears a kilt, and I think
they are, without exception, the most strenuous supporters of Scottish customs I
have ever met. The young ladies, who had always been associated in our minds
with silk dresses and thin shoes, came to call clad in the very shortest and roughest
tweed skirts that I have ever seen; and old Mr. Finlayson, whose mother was a Rob-
inson, has discovered that that is pretty much the same as being a Robertson, and
that therefore, in some mysterious way, he is entitled to wear the Macdonald tartan. They asked us to tea in a very polite and friendly way, and the old rooms were
shown off to us with a good deal of pride. The architecture of the house seemed to
throw a reflected glory on Mr. Finlayson.

'Pure Early Scottish,' he said, pointing to the tall narrow windows with their
shelving ledges.

'So dangerous,' said Mrs. Finlayson, 'for the servants cleaning the windows.'

The drawing-room vases were all filled with heather, and the room smelt of
damp dog and herrings. The Miss Finlaysons came in to tea in thick skirts and
brogues, and they wore tartan tam-o'-shanters very becomingly placed upon their
heads, and affixed to their hair with ornamental bonnet pins. They ate cake with
damp red hands, and seemed to pride themselves upon the fish-scales which still
clung to their skirts, and imparted the rather unpleasant odour which I noticed in
the room. Young Finlayson, in his kilt, showed a great expanse of red knee, and

told tales of remarks made to him by the boatmen, which he considered equal to anything in Ian Maclaren's books.

Mrs. Finlayson took us out after tea to see the garden and tennis court and the game larder. 'I always like a walled garden,' she said, 'it is so stylish.' Mr. Finlayson found a reflected glory even in the loch and the hills, and he waved his fat hand towards them and said: 'We are able to do you a nice bit of view here, aren't we?'

'I tell papa,' said Mrs. Finlayson, 'that he will ruin the girls for anything else after this. The only thing we regret is the want of society. However, a few of the best people round about have called, and we are giving, quite an informal little dinner-party to-morrow night.'

Mrs. Finlayson then invited us to dinner, and when we hesitated, on the plea that we should have one or two friends with us, Mrs. Finlayson, in the most hospitable manner possible, said that she always had a 'profusion on their own table,' so there was nothing for it but to accept her invitation.

The dinner was one of those rather purposeless feasts which are given in the country, and the Finlaysons' neighbours who had been bidden to it bore upon their faces the peculiarly homeless look which one observes in the expressions of one's men friends especially, when they go out to a rural dinner. The look that says as plainly as possible that they are moving about in worlds not realized nor found particularly comfortable, and that they would infinitely prefer their own arm-chairs at home.

The minister took Palestrina in to dinner, and occupied himself throughout the evening by putting the most searching questions to her of an inquisitive nature. He asked how many servants we had, whether we were satisfied with our cook, where we came from, and why we had come. And he did it all with such keen interest and intelligence, that Palestrina admitted that she really had felt flattered rather than provoked. His friend Evan Sinclair, who, having let his house to the Finlaysons, is living on a little farm close by, contradicted everything that the minister said, and the two quarrelled the whole evening.

Old Tyne Drum, who lives a good many miles away, but who with his wife had already been to call upon us, brewed himself the very largest glasses of whisky-toddy which I have ever seen, even on a big night at mess, and he proposed healths and drank the steaming mixture throughout dinner in a very commendable national spirit. His piper, who stood behind his chair, refused at last to pour out any further libations, and I heard him mutter to himself: 'Ye'll no need tae say that Sandy Macnichol ever helpit ye tae the deil.'

Young Finlayson is always very jocose upon the subject of whisky, as befits his ideas about the Highlands; and even the Misses Finlayson, in their faithful loyalty to all things Scottish, were quite pleased with Tyne Drum's performance, and would have scorned to look as though a whisky-drinking laird were a novelty to them.

Mrs. Finlayson told Thomas, in a very severe manner, and in her platform voice which I always find so impressive, that *she* considered intemperance a sin, but that that was what came of all this nonsense about Scotland. She gave him quite a lecture upon the subject, as though he, being Scottish born, was responsible for the old laird's backsliding.

When the unfortunate old gentleman came into the drawing-room to join the ladies and sat down next him, Mrs. Finlayson looked at Thomas as though she thought he was in some sort to blame for this behaviour.

Tyne Drum dropped heavily on to the ottoman, and I heard him say: 'Do you know my wife?'

'Yes,' replied Thomas. 'I have met her several times since we came to the cottage.'

'Hoo old should ye think she was?' (Tyne Drum is always broadly Doric in his speech.) Thomas calculated that the lady must be a long way the wrong side of sixty, and humbly suggested that she might perhaps be forty-five.

'Presairve us!' said the Laird. 'This lad here says my wife is forty-five!' He began to sob bitterly, and, putting his handkerchief to his eyes, cried: 'My pretty wee Jeannie, my bonnie wee wife, wha daurs tae say ye was forty-five!'

Thomas was so sorry for him and for what he had done, that he did his best to cheer him up by telling him that what he had meant to say was twenty-five; but Tyne Drum was inconsolable, and went to sleep with the tear-drops on his cheeks.

When we got home in the evening Palestrina said: 'We are far behind the Finlaysons in all things Scottish. I shall buy a Harris tweed skirt, and you and Thomas must buy something too.' So we drove down in the coach to the ferry on a very wet and windy day to cross over to the 'toon.'

Our place on the coach was shared with a Scot, who was the most truculent defender of the Free Kirk I have ever met. He argued every single point of his creed, and became quite abusive at last, as he denounced the 'Established' and all who belong to it.

The wind was high as we drove in the coach, and the rain fell heavily once or twice, but the voice of the gentleman rose higher and higher as the rain descended. Hughie, the coachman, chided him with no stint of words, and at every burst of eloquence on the passenger's part he remarked: 'Anither worrd and I'll pit ye in the ditch!'

This method of treating the argumentative passenger suggested the possibility of the coach being overturned in order to punish him, and Palestrina grew alarmed.

'I do hope,' she said to Hughie, 'that you will remember that we are not all Wee Frees, and that therefore we do not all require the same treatment meted out to us.'

The guard at the back of the coach here showed his head over the pile of boxes covered with tarpaulin on the roof, and called out: 'Pit him inside the coach wi' Mrs. Macfadyen, and she'll sort him! She'll gie him the Gaelic!'

Hughie chuckled and remarked: 'Ay, she's the gran' wumman wi' her tongue!' And during the rest of the drive his threats to the eloquent passenger took the form of: 'Anither worrd, and I'll pit ye in wi' Mrs. Macfadyen!'

There was a marked improvement in our friend's behaviour after this. He was in great difficulties when he came to get into the ferry-boat. It was easy enough to throw his first leg over the side while holding on by a thole-pin, but the balance required to convey the remaining limb into the boat was quite out of his power. And having made one or two ineffectual hops on the beach with the shore-loving member, he turned to the boatmen, and said gravely: 'Lift in my leg, Angus! Juist gie me a hand wi' ma last leg!'

Palestrina chose the tweed for our coats and her skirt, and then we walked up to the Castle and called on the Melfords, who told us that Mrs. Fielden was coming to stay with them. They sang her praises, as most people do; she has heaps of friends. Then Palestrina did some shopping at the 'flesher's' and the baker's, and we went down to the ferry again—a boy behind us laden with queer-looking parcels containing provisions, and Aloa yarn to knit into stockings, and paper-bags with ginger-bread cakes in them. When we got in and sat down under the brown sail of the heavy boat, the two sailors remained in their places and did not show the least sign of getting under way. Thomas said to the elder of the two men, a fine old fellow with a face such as one connects with stories of the Covenanters:

'Why don't you get off?'

And the old man replied unmoved, 'I'm waiting for the Lord.'

Palestrina, who is sympathetic in every matter, put on an expression of deep religious feeling, and we thought of the Irvingites, and wished that we had Eliza Jamieson with us 'to look it up.' As far as we knew, the Irvingites wait to perform every action until inspired to perform it. We had heard that in the smallest matter, such as beginning to eat their dinner, they will wait until this inspiration, as I suppose one must call it, is given to them. The question then arose, how long would it be before we would be likely to get under way? The two sailors sat on without moving, and the elder of them cut a wedge of tobacco and was filling his pipe preparing to smoke. We wondered if the Irvingites often waited for an inspiration in this contented way. The big red-funnelled steamer from Greenock was, meanwhile, preparing to depart. It had poured its daily output of tourists for their half hour's run in the town, which time they employ in buying mementos of the place, and we had hurried down to the sailing-boat to escape this influx.

Thomas endeavoured to assist inspiration by saying it didn't seem much use waiting any longer, and that as time was getting on, did not our friend (the gray-bearded Covenanter) think that it was time to be moving? The Covenanter wrinkled up his nose, which already was a good deal wrinkled, and gazed upwards at the sail or, as we interpreted it, to Heaven. Palestrina pressed Thomas's hand and said gently, 'Don't urge him, dear, we shall get off in time.' And the younger sailor said, 'We are waiting for the Lord.' So we knew that they were both Irvingites, and the only scepticism that intruded itself upon us was this: Suppose inspiration never came, how should we get home?

The steamer now began to move away from the pier, with a great churning and hissing of water, and seething white foam fizzing round the staples of the pier. A band began to play on board, and the paddles broke the water with a fine sweep. Two youngsters on shore, to whom 'the stimmer' is a daily excitement, then called put in shrill, high voices: 'There's the Lord! She's aff!'

The *Lord of the Isles* had moved off on her return journey to Greenock, and the notes on Scottish religion which Palestrina was carefully preparing were hastily destroyed. The *Lord* had departed, and we sailed across the loch without waiting any longer.

When we got home, we found the minister awaiting us in the drawing-room, he having suggested that as we were not at home, he had better stay till our return. I found out in the course of conversation, that he is a distant relation of old Captain Jamieson—the Jamiesons' father—so we had quite a long talk about our friends. The minister is one of those Scots whose national characteristics are always stronger than individual character. Take away his nationality from him, and Mr. Macorquodale would be nothing at all. His qualities being entirely Scottish, it is only logical to assume that if Mr. Macorquodale were not Scottish, he would be non-existent.

Palestrina came out on to the little terrace where we were sitting, and I explained to her that the minister was a cousin of the Jamiesons.

'How interesting!' said Palestrina, in her usual kind way.

'Why?' said the minister. He has sandy hair and very round gray eyes, and looks like a football player.

'Oh, I don't know,' said my sister; 'it's always interesting, isn't it, to find that people are related?'

'Everyone must have some relations,' said Mr. Macorquodale, 'and if my choice had been given me, I do not think I should have chosen those five gurrls.'

'We like them so much,' Palestrina said, smiling.

'Is that the truth?' said Mr. Macorquodale; and she replied firmly that it was.

'Um umph!' he said, as though considering a perfectly new problem, and then added: 'Well, each man to his taste. How many of them have got husbands?'

I replied that Kate was married and Gracie engaged.

'Gracie?' said the minister simply. 'Was that the one with a nose like a scone?'

We considered Gracie's nose silently for a moment, and then admitted that perhaps the simile was not unjust.

'How did she get him?' said the minister presently.

The minister has a curious way of eating, which fascinates one to look at, while all the time there is a distinct feeling that an accident may happen at any moment. When tea was brought out he accepted some, and filled his mouth very full of cookie, stowing into it nearly a whole one at a time, and then raised his tea-cup to his lips. He persists in keeping his spoon in his cup as he drinks, and he prevents it from tumbling out by holding it with his thumb. A long draught of tea is then partaken of with a gurgling sound, and the minister swallows audibly. It is almost impossible to prevent one's self watching this process of eating and drinking during the whole of tea-time. For it seems so uncertain whether the spoon will remain in its place, and the cookie and the tea.

The minister is a very young man, with the pugnacity of an Edinburgh High School boy, and the awful truthfulness which distinguishes his nation, but which is accentuated in such an alarming degree in a minister of the Kirk.

'I sent Kate a scent-bottle when she married,' he remarked. 'I won it at a bazaar for sixpence, so it was not expensive. I don't disapprove of raffles," he added, although he had not been asked for this piece of information—'that is, if ladies do not cheat over it, as they often do.' Palestrina bristled at the insinuation, and the minister consoled her by saying: 'Women sin in such wee ways—that's what I can't understand about them. However,' he said, 'I have never known a woman steal a thing yet, that a man has not reaped some benefit by it. I can quote authority for my views from Adam and Eve downwards, to the newspapers of yesterday. I am engaged to be married myself, and I find the subject of feminine ethics absorbing. Good-bye,' he said presently, 'I hope you will not be disappointed with the clothes I hear you've ordered.'

Alas! the tweed coat and skirt in which my sister hoped to rival the Miss Finlaysons, proved an utter misfit, and she drove round the loch on the following day to take the garments back. Palestrina had prepared a severe reprimand for the tailor, but the old man took the wind out of her sails by stopping in amazement at the first word of annoyance which she uttered, and standing in the middle of the little fitting-room, with a yellow tape measure round his neck, and a piece of chalk in his hand, he shook his gray beard at us with something of Apostolic fervour, and thus addressed us:

'I'm amazed at ye! Do ye ever consider the system of planets, and that this world is one of the lesser points of light in space, and that even here there are countless millions of human beings, full of great resolves and high purposes. Get outside yourselves, ladies and gentlemen, and realize in the magnitude of the universe, and the immeasurable majesty of the planetary system, how small a thing is the ill-fit of a jacket.'

We felt much humbled, Palestrina and I. And it was only when we were driving home afterwards, that it even dimly suggested itself to us that we had right on our side at all. 'After all,' Palestrina said, 'the coats did not fit; I really do not think he need have lectured us so severely.'

At the time, however, I confess that our feelings were distinctly apologetic.

One wonders how a tailor who advanced the planetary system as a reproof to complaining customers, would get on in London, and one realizes that English people have a great deal still to learn.

CHAPTER XVIII

WHEN Mrs. Fielden came to stay at the Melfords we saw a good deal of her. Their yacht used to steam up in the early morning, and they would take us off for a day's cruise on the loch or for a trip round to Oban. Mrs. Fielden used to sit on deck with a big red umbrella over her head and a white yachting gown on, and seemed serenely unconscious that she was looking very pretty and very smart. My sister tells me she never feels badly dressed till she meets Mrs. Fielden.

The Melfords have very pleasant people stopping with them always, and there are very jolly little parties on board their yacht. Mrs. Fielden, however, is in her most provoking and wilful mood. Every day it is the same thing—laughter and smiles for everyone. But she has absolutely no heart. All the beautiful, kindly things she does are only the whim of the moment. They bespeak a generous nature, as easily moved to tears as to laughter; but she loves everyone a little, and probably has no depth of affection or constancy in her. Lately, she has added another provoking habit to the many she already possesses. She exaggerates her pretence of having no memory, and indeed it may be she has not any.

When I left home, rather a wreck as regards health, and drove to the station in Mrs. Fielden's luxurious carriage, it was her hand that piled the cushions as no one else can, behind me. And the last thing I saw was her smile as she waved her hand to me from my own door.

Last week, when we met again at the Melfords', she nodded to me in a little indifferent sort of way. She sat under a big cedar-tree on one of the lawns, and laughed, and talked a sort of brilliant nonsense the whole afternoon.

By-and-by I said to her—probably clumsily, certainly at the wrong time—'I never half thanked you for being so good to me when I was ill;' for she had come in like some radiant vision, day after day, in her beautiful summer gowns and rose-garlanded hats, and had sat by my couch, reading to me sometimes, talking to me at others in a voice as gentle as a dove's.

Why will she not allow one to admire her? One only wants to do so humbly and at a distance. It was so pleasant up here in the Highlands, with the dear memory of those long days to look back upon. But Mrs. Fielden ruthlessly robbed me and sent me away empty the very first day of our meeting.

'Was I kind to you? I don't believe I was, really. If I was, I'm sure I forget all about it. Let me see, how long were you ill? It can't have been a bit amusing for you,' and so on, laughing at my dull face and serious ways.

And this has gone on for a whole week. At the Melfords' parties she selects, quite indiscriminately, and in a royal way which she has got, this man or that to be her escort or her companion. Now it is a mere boy whom she bewilders with a few of her radiant smiles, and now one of her elderly Colonels whom she reduces to a state of abject admiration in a few hours. One man goes fishing with her, and another rows her on the loch. A third, hearing that Mrs. Fielden's life will be a blank if she does not possess a certain rare fern which may be found sometimes on the hillsides of Scotland, spends a whole day scrambling about looking for it, and returns triumphant in the evening. Mrs. Fielden has forgotten that she ever wanted it. When we sulk she does not notice it. When her Colonels offer her their fatuous admiration she goes to sleep, and then, waking up, is so very, very sorry. 'But you can't have amused me properly,' she says, 'or I should have stayed awake.' When anyone tries, by avoiding her, to show displeasure, Mrs. Fielden is oblivious of the fact. And when the penitence and boredom which immediately ensue when one has deprived Mrs. Fielden of one's company, have led one to end the one-sided quarrel with an apology, it is only to find that Mrs. Fielden has been blissfully unconscious of one's absence. Summer and the air of the Highlands seem to be in her veins. Her happiness, like the quality of mercy, is twice blessed, making her, through her talent for enjoyment, diffuse something beautiful and gay about her.

After all, why should she care? Life was evidently made to give her pleasure. Why should a woman always be blamed for being loved? Mrs. Fielden's charm is of the irresponsible sort. To live and to be lovely are all one ought to demand of her, and at least she is without vanity. She seems to be entirely unconscious of the admiration she receives, or perhaps she is simply indifferent to it.

The Melfords adore her, and allow her to see it. They say no one knows her as they do. Probably we all feel that. This is one of Mrs. Fielden's most maddening charms. We have all found something in her that seems to belong to ourselves alone.

Lately I have discovered that she loves to wander up the hillside by herself, and listen to the plover's solitary cry, and sit in the sunshine with no companion near her. And one wonders why so frivolous a woman should care for this, and why when she comes back amongst us again, her eyes should wear the wistful look which covers them like a veil sometimes.

When she left the Melfords', Palestrina asked her to come and stay with us, and rather to my surprise, Mrs. Fielden came. It seems to me she must find us a very dull lot after the Melfords' cheery house-parties. She arrived late one afternoon in the yacht, and the whole party came up to dine with us before returning to the castle. The little house was taxed to its utmost capacity, even to provide teacups for our guests. But the Melfords have a happy knack of seeming to find pleasure in everything. Mrs. Fielden's gaiety was infectious, and her lightheadedness knocked all one's serious world to pieces, while her beauty seemed almost extravagant in the plain setting of the little house.

She began to give us some of her experiences in Scotland. 'Do you know,' she said, putting on a charming gravity and lifting her eyebrows in a provoking, childish way, 'that every single person in Scotland gets up at five o'clock in the morning? and all the coaches and excursions start at daybreak, and when you want to hit off what they call a "connection "anywhere, you have to get up in the middle of the night?'

'I am afraid you had a horribly early start to join the yacht the other day,' said Lord Melford, 'but it was the only way we could manage to get to the Oban Gathering in time.'

'I was there before you,' said Mrs. Fielden; 'and I had to rouse up the people at the inn to take me in and give me breakfast. Even they were not up at that hour! But after ringing twice, such a nice boots came and opened the door to me and brought me some breakfast.'

'The gathering was very good this year,' said Lord Melford. 'Why didn't some of you come? By-the-by, your friend Mrs. Macdonald was there. Indeed, it was she who insisted on taking Mrs. Fielden to the Gaelic concert.'

'Gaelic is rather an alarming language,' said Mrs. Fielden. 'I always feel as if I were being sworn at when I hear it.'

One of Mrs. Fielden's admirers, who had reached the savage and sarcastic stage, here interposed, and said: 'Poor Mrs. Fielden! I saw you at the concert. How did you manage to sit throughout a whole evening between Mrs. Macdonald and a wall?'

'Mrs. Macdonald is quite a dear!' said Mrs. Fielden. (Who, in the name of Fortune, would Mrs. Fielden not find charming?)

'I don't know what you and Mrs. Macdonald can have found to talk about,' said Palestrina, laughing.

'We discussed the training of servants most of the time,' said Mrs. Fielden simply.

Everyone laughed; and my sister, with a recollection of our visit to Mrs. Macdonald, said at once: 'Did she give you any useful household recipes?'

'It is very odd that you should have asked me that,' said Mrs. Fielden. 'Do you know, that the whole of to-day I have been puzzling over a letter which I received this morning? I did not know the handwriting, and it was merely headed: "Two recipes for boiling a ham, as requested." Now, I cannot really have asked Mrs. Macdonald for recipes for boiling a ham, can I?'

We thought it highly probable that she had done so, and had done it, too, with an air of profound interest; and I think we said this, which Mrs. Fielden did not mind in the least.

'There is something rather horrible, don't you think so,' she said, 'in knowing how a thing is cooked?'

The minister, who is assiduous in calling, walked up after tea with his friend Evan Sinclair; and as we were already far too large a party for dinner, we asked them to stay too.

Mr. Macorquodale has frequently described himself to us as a grand preacher. He and Evan Sinclair live quite close to each other, and they are friends whose affection is rooted and maintained in warfare. For the minister and Sinclair to meet is one strenuous contest as to who shall have the last word. Politeness is not a strong motive with either of them—indeed, one would imagine that from the first it has been ruled out of place. The friendship and the warfare began at the Edinburgh High School years ago, and both the friendship and the warfare have lasted without intermission ever since. They meet every day, and often twice a day; they fish together, and in the winter they spend every evening with each other. Scottish people seem to have a sneaking liking for those who dislike them, and a certain pity mingled with contempt for those who show them favour and affection. The friendship of Evan and the minister is based upon feelings of the most respectful admiration for their mutual antipathy.

To keep alive this laudable and self-respecting warfare, is the highest effort of genius of both Mr. Sinclair and the Reverend Alexander. To foster it they apply themselves to what they call 'plain speaking' whenever they meet, and they conceal as much as possible from each other every single good quality that they possess.

The minister, who is a big man, always talks of Evan as 'Wee Sinkler,' and sneers at 'heritors'; and Evan invariably addresses Macorquodale as 'Taurbarrels,' a name which he considers appropriate to the minister's black clothes and portly figure.

'The minister,' said Evan, when he had walked up the hill to see us, 'has been reading Josephus. We shall have some erudite learning from the pulpit for the next Sunday or two.'

The minister was announced a moment later, and, before taking the trouble to shake hands with us, he looked Evan Sinclair over from top to toe, and remarked: 'Ye're very attentive in calling upon ladies.'

'I was just talking about your fine preaching,' said Evan.

'I admit my gift,' said the minister; 'but I fear that I very often preach to a deaf adder which stops its ears.' He nodded triumphantly at us, and it then occurred to him to shake hands.

Evan said at once that he got a better sleep in kirk on Sundays than he got during the whole of the week.

'Evan Sinclair,' said the minister, 'if I find you sleeping under me, I'll denounce you from my pulpit, as a minister has the right to do.'

'And we'll settle it in the graveyard afterwards,' said Evan drily. 'And ye're not in very good training, my man.'

Palestrina broke in gently to discuss a theological point which had puzzled us for several Sundays. On each Lord's Day as it came round we had prayed that we might become 'a little beatle to the Lord.' Doubtless the simile is a beautiful one, but its immediate bearing upon our needs was not too grossly evident. And it seemed almost dangerous to those who believe in the efficacy of prayer to put up this petition in its literal sense. We had decided for some time past, that we should ask Mr. Macorquodale what it was exactly for which we made petition, when we prayed that we might become a 'little beatle to the Lord.'

Similes,' said Palestrina, in her serious way, 'are beautiful sometimes, but we can't quite understand one of the references that you make in your prayers on Sundays.'

We have prayed so fervently,' said Mrs. Fielden,' without, perhaps entirely understanding the portent of the petition, that we might become a "little beatle to the Lord."'

The thing was out now, and our curiosity, we hoped, would be gratified. There was a pause which suggested that our hearers were puzzled, and then Mr. Sinclair put a large pocket-handkerchief into his mouth and roared with laughter, and Mr. Macorquodale turned to my sister, who was trembling now, and remarked in an awful voice, that he wondered that we didn't understand plain English.

Of course she apologized, and an explanation came afterwards from Evan Sinclair, who told us that the minister's prayer was that we—the church—might become a little Bethel, and that Beethel was his Doric pronunciation of the word.

It began to rain on Sunday, as it often does in Scotland—Nature itself seems to put on a more serious expression on the Sabbath—and it continued raining for four whole days. The rain came down steadily and mercilessly, shutting out the view of the hills, and turning the whole landscape into a big damp gray blanket. 'I suppose,' said Mrs. Fielden, who is never affected by bad weather, 'that we shall all get very cross and quarrel with each other, if the rain continues much longer.'

'I think I shall write a number of unnecessary letters to absent friends,' said

Palestrina. 'And Mr. Ellicomb and Sir Anthony Crawshay will arrive to-morrow, and we must tell them to amuse us.'

It was a disappointment to find that Mr. Elli-comb's nerves and temper were seriously affected by the weather, and in moments of extreme depression his low spirits vented themselves in a rabid abuse of the Presbyterian Kirk. I cannot understand why Ellicomb should elect to wear a brown velvet shooting-jacket, and a pale-green tie, and neat boots laced halfway up his leg, in Scotland. He went to the village church in the rain on Sunday, and he has not been the same man since.

'Don't call it a church!' he cried, as we went homewards up the hill, where the road was a watercourse and each tree poured down moisture. He seemed to think that he had done his soul an irreparable injury by entering a Presbyterian kirk.

Anthony said: 'Oh! don't be an ass, Ellicomb.' But even on Monday morning, poor Ellicomb was still suffering from the weather and the effects of his church-going.

'Can he be in love?' said Palestrina; 'and if so, as the Jamiesons would say, which is it?'

Palestrina is prettier than ever since her marriage. She still says: 'Oh, that will be delightful!' to whatever Thomas and I suggest, and she never seems to have any occupation except to be with us when we want her, and to accede to everything we say, which of course, from a man's point of view, is a very delightful trait in a woman.

'I rather wonder,' said Palestrina, 'that I have not heard from any of the Jamiesons lately. They are usually such good writers.'

'Depend upon it, there is a great bit of news coming,' said Thomas. 'The Jamiesons always maintain a dramatic silence just before announcing some tremendous piece of intelligence.'

Thomas had hardly spoken the words before a telegram was handed to Palestrina, containing the following enigmatical words:

Engaged Cuthbertson. Greatly surprised. Deeply thankful.—ELIZA.'

This rather mysterious message was followed, later in the day, by a letter four pages in length, and marked on the outside, for some reason best known to Eliza, 'Immediate.' The letter explained more fully the cause of Eliza's thankfulness, and who it was that was greatly surprised.

'If you had told me,' wrote Eliza, 'six weeks ago, that I should now be engaged to Mr. Cuthbertson, I should hardly have believed it. I really had not a notion that he cared for me until he actually said the words. Is it not too strange, to think that perhaps after all, Maud may be one of the last of us to get married?'

Here followed the usual descriptive catalogue, so characteristic of the Jamiesons' letters. 'Mr. Cuthbertson looks like a widower, though he is not one.' Strangely enough, I could never think of any other words, when I came to know Mr. Cuthbertson, that described him so well as these, and I can only account for it by saying that the man's deep melancholy and the crape band that he habitually wore round his hat, must have given one the feeling that at some time Mr. Cuthbertson must have suffered a heavy bereavement. 'I have only known him,' Eliza's letter went on, 'for six weeks, but even that time has shown me his worth. He has a very straight nose and a black beard, and his forehead is distinctly intellectual. I met him first at Mrs. Darcey-Jacobs', where, as you know, I had gone to stay to catalogue their library, and to do a little typewriting for her. You know, of course, that she has become a member of the S.R.S., and their library is a *mine of information.*

'At first I was afraid to say, or even to allow myself to think, he showed me any preference, but Maud thought from the first that he was struck, and I asked her not to appear at all until everything was settled, for you know how attractive she is. But I really don't think that even then I thought that there was anything serious in it.' (For an intelligent woman, Eliza's letter strikes one as being strangely lacking in concentration.) 'I have just been to the meeting of the Browning Society—our first appearance in public together—and I read my paper on "The Real Strafford," but I could hardly keep my voice steady all the time. I wear his own signet-ring for the present, but we are going up to London next week, when he will buy me a hoop of pearls. I am sure that you will be glad to hear that he is comfortably off. When the right man comes, preconceived objections to matrimony vanish, *but it must be the right man.'*

Palestrina said that she was 'thrilled' to hear of Eliza's engagement, because an engagement was always thrilling, and she instantly went to tell the news to Mr. Ellicomb. She told me afterwards that when she had said that one of the Jamiesons was engaged, Mr. Ellicomb became suddenly very pale in his complexion, and exclaimed, in a most anxious tone of voice: 'Which?'

The cold weather has set in very suddenly, and already there is a sprinkling of snow on some of the distant hills. The robins still sing cheerily, but the gulls on the shore, flying over the yellow seaweed, call to each other plaintively in the gray of the early twilight. The heavy-winged herons stand in an attitude of serious thought for hours on the cold rocks; then, as if suddenly making up their minds to something, they stretch out their red legs behind them, and flop with large wings over the waters of the loch. The red Virginian creeper has begun to drop its leaves regretfully, after a night or two of white frost, and the dahlias hang their heads, heavy with the moisture which their cups contain. The sun wakes late in the mornings now, but shines strong and warm when it does get up. Cottage lights and fires burn cheerily o' nights, and within the cottages the old folks and the young ones draw round the fires and speak eerily of wraiths and whaurlochs, and some will tell of death-lights which they have seen on the lonely shore road. The herring fishers, who sail away in the early twilight, wear good stout jerseys now and red woollen 'crauvats,' which the 'wumman at hame' has knitted. The **Lord** has sailed away to Dunoon to lay up for the winter, and the shepherds have gone away down South 'to winter the hogs.' The shepherds' wives sit alone in the little hillside cottages away up on the face of the brae, and 'mak dae' with their slender money till their men come home again.

The old women in the village have begun their winter spinning, and the tap, tap, tap of the treadle on the floor, gives a pleasant sound as one passes outside on the dark road. Old men tell tales of snow in the passes in winter-time, and of death on the bleak hillsides, and some wife, shuddering, will say, 'Aye, I mind I saw his corp-licht the very evening he was lost.' And then they tell tales of fantasy and signs and premonitions of death.

The Finlaysons are going to wind up their very successful autumn in the Highlands by giving what they insist upon calling a gillies' dance, though probably the revels will mostly be indulged in by their large retinue of English servants. Good-natured old Finlayson has more than once said that he hopes we shall all come to the gillies' dance, and that it will give ourselves and our guests a chance of seeing some Highland customs. A good many of us come to Scotland most years, and have seen gillies and pipers before, but our good-natured neighbours certainly out-distance anyone I know in their Highland sympathies.

They invited us to dine with them before the dance should begin, and six of us went, feeling very like the Jamiesons, and resolved that when we got home we should never put a limit to their numbers when we send them an invitation again.

We talk of returning home at the end of next week, and Mrs. Fielden and our other two guests are leaving on Monday, I believe.

Mrs. Fielden looks much prettier in the Highlands, I think, than anywhere else. Young Finlayson is in love with her, and I believe has offered her his heart and the ironmongery business with it; but I think of all her lovers Anthony Crawshay is the one she likes best. He is the only one for whom her moods never alter, and to whom she is always gracious and charming and sweet. Perhaps it is in a quiet, less radiant way than that in which she treats others, but it is with an unvarying loving-kindness which I have not seen her bestow elsewhere. And Anthony Crawshay is a good fellow—one of the best.

Old Mr. Finlayson actually donned a kilt for the gillies' dance; young Finlayson also wore the national dress, and Thomas tells me that they have sported the Macdonald tartan, and wants to know why. Old Finlayson met us at the door of his baronial hall in a clannish, feudal sort of way, and seizing his glengarry bonnet from his head, he flung it down upon the oak settle in the hall, and exclaimed, in hearty accents: 'Welcome to the Glen.' The Misses Finlayson wore sashes of royal Stuart tartan put plaidwise across their shoulders. Mrs. Finlayson was dressed in a very regal manner, which I cannot attempt to describe, and her platform voice was in use throughout the entire evening.

Ellicomb said the dance was barbaric, but Thomas enjoyed the evening immensely, and so did Crawshay, who said in his hearty way: 'The Finlaysons did us uncommonly well,' and shouted out, 'Not at all bad people, not at all bad.'

After dinner, old Finlayson showed us all the pictures in the hall by the light of a long wax taper which he held above his head, and he pointed out the beauties of the house in a proprietary way, even to Evan himself, to whom the place belongs. Evan Sinclair, in a shabby green doublet, accepted all Mr. Finlayson's wildest statements about his own house with a queer, humorous grin on his face, and submitted to being patronized by the Miss Finlaysons, whose commercial instincts, no doubt, caused them to despise a young man who was obliged to let his place.

One of the Highland axioms which the Finlaysons have accepted is that 'a man's a man for a' that,' and they shook hands with everyone in an effusive way, and condescended to a queer sort of familiarity with the boatmen and keepers about the place. The daughters of the house, with flying tartan ribbons, swung the young ghillies about in the intricate figures of the hoolichan, and talked to them with a heartiness which one would hardly have thought possible of the Clarkham young ladies. The Finlaysons had a large number of English guests staying in the house for the dance. These all made the same joke when the pipes began to play. 'Is the pig being killed?' they asked, and looked very pleased with their own ready wit.

Red-headed Evan Sinclair carried his old green doublet and battered silver ornaments very well, and his neat dancing was in pleasant contrast to the curious bounds and leaps of the Finlaysons. Old Mr. Finlayson spent his evening strutting about in a kindly, important fashion, and in making Athole Brose after a recipe supplied by Tyne Drum, who superintended the brewing of it himself.

I hope I am not fanciful when I say that the pipes when I hear them, have to me something irresistibly sad about them, and that they conjure up many fantasies in my head which I am half ashamed to put down on paper. They seem to me to gather up in their bitter sobbings all the sorrows of a people who have suffered much and have said very little about it. There is the cry in them of children dying in the lonely glens in winter-time, when the wind howls round the clachan and the snow fills the passes. One almost sees the little procession of black-coated men bearing away a tiny burden from the cottage door into the whiteness beyond, with its one heaped-up patch of brown earth on either side of the little grave. They wail, too, of the Killing Time, when the Covenanters were crushed, but never broken, under persecution; and one seems to see the defiant gray-haired old men, with their splendid obstinacy, unmoved by threats—not defiant, but simply unbreakable. Thinking of the Covenanters as they pass slowly before one to the sighing of the pipes, one wonders if it is possible to punish by death the man who is content to die?

The tuneful reeds sob out, too, the story of the Prince for whom so many brave men bled, and they tell again of the days of song, and of noble legends and deeds of daring, when the nation spent its passionate love on its King. 'Come back! come back!' The desolate cry of the times. Almost one seems to hear it sounding across the hills, and it seems to me that all that it is so hard to speak, so hard even to look, may perhaps be told in music. And I think loyalty and love speak very beautifully in the old Jacobite airs.

Again, as Evan's piper marches up and down in the moonlight playing a lament, the romance of life seems lost in the hardness of it, its stress and its loss. 'Hame, hame, hame!' the pipes sob forth, crying for the homes that are sold to strangers, and for the hills and the glens which pass away from the old hands. It is 'Good-bye, good-bye,' an eternity of farewells. And still, wherever life is most difficult, comforts most few, work most hard, in the distant parts of the world, are the Scottish exiles. But I know that all the world over, the sons of the heather and the mist, in however distant or alien lands they may be, feel always, as they steer their way through life, that there is a pole-star by which they set their compass; and that some day, perhaps, they or their children may steer the boat to a haven on some rocky shore, where the whaup calls shrilly on the moors above the loch, and the heather grows strong and tough on the hillside, and the peat reek rises, almost like the incense of an evening prayer, against a gray, soft sky in the land of the North.

I suppose that even in a diary I have no business to mix this up with an account of the Finlaysons' dance.

Palestrina came up to me, after conscientiously dancing reels with Thomas, looking very pink and pretty, and thoughtful of me, as usual.

'Don't stay longer than you feel inclined,' she said. 'I told them to come for you in the dog-cart, and to wait about for you between twelve and one.'

'I will take a turn down on the shore,' I said, 'and have a cigar, and then I will come back and see how you are getting on.'

Palestrina gave me my crutch, and I went down towards the loch, which looked like a sheet of silver in the moonlight, and I found Anthony and Mrs. Fielden sitting on a garden bench beneath some wind-torn beeches by the shore. To-night there was not a breath of air stirring, and Mrs. Fielden had only thrown a light wrap round her.

'Have you come to tell me that I am to go in and dance reels with old Mr. Finlayson?' she said. 'It is really so much pleasanter out here. Do sit down and talk to Sir Anthony and me.'

(She would never have allowed one to know that one was in the way, even if one had interrupted a proposal of marriage.)

Anthony made room for me on the bench, and said heartily: 'I am awfully glad to see you able to sit up like this, Hugo. Why, man, you're getting as strong as a horse!'

'Oh, I'm all right again,' I said. 'I'll begin to grow a new leg soon. And the first thing I mean to do when that happens, is to dance reels like the Finlaysons.'

'I believe I ought to be going in to supper now with Mr. Finlayson,' said Mrs. Fielden. 'Does anyone know what time it is? He said he would "conduct me to the dining - hall" at twelve o'clock.'

'It is a quarter past now,' said Anthony, looking at his watch in the moonlight. 'Don't go in, Mrs. Fielden. Wait out here, and talk to Hugo and me.'

But old Finlayson, in his kilt, had tracked us to our seat underneath the beech-trees, and he took instant possession of our fair neighbour, and told us to follow presently. He thought all the supper-tables were full just now.

'We shan't eat everything before you come,' said hospitable old Finlayson, walking away with his beautiful partner on his arm.

Mrs. Fielden was dressed in white satin, with some pretty soft stuff about her, and she wore some white heather in her hair.

'What a good sort she is!' said Anthony, in a loud voice, almost before Mrs. Fielden was out of hearing. It wasn't, perhaps, the most poetical way that he could have put it, but one didn't want or expect Anthony to express himself poetically.

'Utterly spoilt!' I replied, because at that moment I happened to be feeling supremely miserable, and I did not want Anthony to know it.

'Not a bit,' he replied; 'and you know that as well as I do, old chap.'

'Allow me, Anthony,' I said, 'to be as savage as I like; it is one of the privileges of a cripple.'

'Oh, blow cripples!' said Anthony. 'You will be shooting next autumn, man.'

'And what will you be doing?' I said. After all, we have been pals all our lives, and I think Anthony might tell me about it if there is anything to tell.

'Oh, I'll be shooting too, I suppose,' said Anthony. We smoked for some time in silence.

And then Anthony began, and said that he had enjoyed himself amazingly up here in the North, and he went on to say a good word for everyone. Old Finlayson had been a brick about his shooting and deer-stalking, and it was beastly hard luck that I hadn't been able to come too. The minister wasn't a bad fellow, even when he was jocose, and Evan Sinclair was one of the best: and so on.

'What shall you be doing when you go back, Anthony?' I said, harking back to my old question, and hoping for more information than I actually asked for. 'Are you going straight home?'

'I'll be at the first shoot at Stanby. Shall you be there?'

'I'm afraid not,' I said. 'I haven't learned to do cross-stitch yet, and I'm sure all the women would think me a great bore, sitting about in their morning-rooms all day. Except Mrs. Fielden, of course! Mrs. Fielden would probably persuade me into thinking that the only thing that made her house-party successful, or had saved herself from boredom, was the presence of a lame man in the house.'

'I don't think you are quite just about Mrs. Fielden, Hugo,' said Anthony, moving rather resentfully on the garden bench.

'That doesn't matter much,' I replied. 'One voice will not be missed much from the general chorus of praise that follows Mrs. Fielden wherever she goes.'

'No; but still—' began Anthony; and then he stopped, and we smoked on for some time without speaking. 'You see,' he began at last, 'she is the best friend I ever had.' He did not lower his voice, because I suppose Anthony finds it impossible to do so, but went on steadily: 'You see, I once cared for a little cousin of hers, and she died when she was eighteen. I don't think anybody ever knew about it, except Mrs. Fielden. But she knows how much cut up I was, and I suppose that is why she is so nice to me always.'

'I'm awfully sorry!' I said.

'I never meant to speak about it,' said Anthony, in a brisk, cheerful voice. 'Oh, don't you bother about it, Hugo! I mean I'm awfully keen about hunting, and I have an excellent time, only I don't suppose I shall ever care for anyone else.'

'Thanks for telling me, Tony.'

'I wouldn't have said anything about it,' said Anthony,' if it hadn't been for what you said about Mrs. Fielden. Y'see, she has been so awfully good to me, and I don't think you quite understand all she is really.'

'Why, man,' I cried, 'I love her with every bit of my heart! And I worship her—how does one say one worships a woman?—as if she were the sun!'

And I think that was the very first moment that I knew I loved Mrs. Fielden.

CHAPTER XIX

THE minister and Evan Sinclair came to say goodbye; the minister has accepted our approaching departure with his usual philosophy. 'You would soon tire of this place in the winter-time,' he said. 'And even looking at it from the other point of view, I believe that summer visitors should not prolong their stay above a few months. I admit that we have enjoyed your sojourn amongst us; but were you and your sister to become residenters in the place, our intercourse would have to be reconstructed from the foundation.' The minister crossed his legs, and, without being pressed to continue the subject, he went on: 'There is a certain conventionality, not to say forbearance, admitted and allowed between friends with whom one's acquaintance is to be short; but there is a basis stronger than that upon which any lengthy friendship must be made.'

'And that basis?' I asked.

'That basis, I take it,' said the minister, 'should be a straightforward disregard for one another. I do not believe in politeness between near neighbours; it cannot last.'

'I had hoped,' said Palestrina, pouting a little, 'that you would all miss us, Mr. Macorquodale.'

'We shall miss you,' said the minister quickly, but with judgment. We shall see the merits as well as the demerits of the case. 'For instance, one of your friends cost me a sovereign for a favourite charity of hers.'

Evan Sinclair said very kindly, blinking his fair eyelashes in a shy way: 'Well, I know I shall miss you. The place will seem very dull with only Alexander and me left in it.'

' *I* shall have my wife,' said the minister brutally.

'Yes,' said Sinclair; 'and her mother! You have kept that pretty dark from us, Taurbarrels.'

'It is only a visit,' said Mr. Macorquodale shortly. And he went on in a truculent tone: 'And I need not have her unless I want to.'

'I hear she is strict,' murmured Evan. 'I hope you will be allowed to look out of the window on the Sabbath, my man.'

'I am master in my own house,' said Mr. Macorquodale magnificently.

'Believe me,' said Evan, 'that's a courtesy title, supported by no valid claim, and still less precedent. A man never has been master of his own house, when there is a mistress in it. I remember when my brother got married, he had just your very ideas, and he gave his wife the keys of the linen-press and the store cupboard, "But the rest of the bunch," he said, "I keep to myself." And he put them all in his pocket. It was not six months after that,' said Evan, 'that I went to stay with them, and I heard him ask my sister-in-law if she would mind his having two pocket-handker-chiefs on Sundays.'

Palestrina and I were alone, for Ellicomb had left us a few days before, and we hear from the Jamiesons that he is a daily visitor at their house. Thomas and Anthony were out shooting, and Mrs. Fielden had gone for a walk over the hills.

'I have a thousand things to do,' said Palestrina, when Evan and the minister had departed.

'I also have a thousand things to do,' I replied.

'Don't tire yourself,' said Palestrina. 'What are you going to do?'

'I am going to re-write my diary,' I said.

'But, my dear,' said Palestrina, 'that would be the work of months.'

'I am only going to correct all the mistakes I have made in it,' I replied; and I took my book and a pen, and went and sat in the little room on the ground-floor which they call my den.

We once had an old aunt, Palestrina and I, who kept a diary all her life, and when any of the relatives whom she mentioned in its pages came to die, she used to go through all the back numbers of her journal and insert affectionate epithets in front of the names of the deceased. For instance (my aunt's existence was not marked by any thrilling events), the entry would perhaps be as follows: 'Maria was late for breakfast this morning. In the afternoon she had her singing-lesson, and afterwards we did some shopping, when Maria tried on her new gown.' But the amended entry after Maria's death would be, 'Our darling Maria was (a little) late for breakfast this morning; in the afternoon she had her singing-lesson'—and here would probably be a footnote praising Maria's voice—'afterwards we did some shopping, and'—Maria struck out—'my sweet girl tried on her new gown.' Anyone's death, or even a successful marriage of one of the family, would cause her to revise and correct her diary in this way, and she used to fan the wet ink with a piece of blotting-paper to make it dry black, and thus prevent posterity knowing that the words written over the lines were an afterthought induced by subsequent events.

It was manifestly an unfair way of keeping a diary. But I can claim her example, and hereditary taint, as an excuse for my own dishonesty this afternoon. I read through my diary with a sense of utter shame, and wherever I found, for instance, that I had said that Mrs. Fielden was frivolous, or even that she raised her eyebrows in an affected way, I corrected the misstatement by the light of the magnificent discovery I had made, that Mrs. Fielden was faultless, and that I loved her. Oh! the beauty of this woman and her blessed kindness! the cunning with which she conceals her unselfishness, and her ridiculous attempts at pretending she is frivolous or worldly.

Alas! there were so many misstatements to correct, and so many dear adjectives to fill in, that I was not halfway through my task, before Mrs. Fielden herself tapped at the window and looked in.

I believe I must have grinned foolishly, but what I wanted to do was to stretch out my arms to the beautiful vision, framed in the hectic Virginian creeper round the window, and call out to her to come to me.

Mrs. Fielden came in for a minute and said, with the adorable lift of the eyebrows: 'I have been educating a pair of young boots by walking through all the bogs on the hillside. Listen, they are quite full of water.' She raised herself on her toes with a squelching sound of the leather, and gave one of her joyous soft laughs.

'You must change directly,' I said, with an idiotic sense of proprietorship.

'When I have done so, I think I shall come and have tea with you,' said Mrs. Fielden. And of course then I knew that she had come home early on purpose to have tea with me, and that probably she had given up something else which she wanted to do, in order that she might sit by me when I was alone—because of course I have found Mrs. Fielden out now, and exposed her hypocrisy.

Fortunately, she took nearly a quarter of an hour to change her wet boots, and this gave me time to ask myself why I was behaving like a raving idiot, because I had found out that Mrs. Fielden was absolutely perfect, and that I loved her.

It was quite the worst quarter of an hour that I have ever spent, because in it I had time to remember that I was a crippled man with one leg, and that Mrs. Fielden was a beautiful young woman, whom of course everyone loved, and that she owned an old historical place called Stanby, and probably—I realized this also—that she would continue to come over and sit with a dull man and bewilder him with her beauty and her kindness, only so long as he did not allow her to know the supremely impertinent fact that he had fallen in love with her.

I must plead ill-health, and a certain weakness of nerve, which no doubt always follows a surgical operation, for the fact that I turned round and put my face in the pillows for a moment and groaned.

Mrs. Fielden came in my favourite pale blue gown, which she sometimes wears when she changes her frock at tea-time. She came and took a chair beside me, and as she never hurriedly plunges into a conversation, we sat silent for a time. The afternoon was darkening now, and the light of a blazing fire leaped and played upon her pale blue dress, and turned her brown hair to a sort of red-gold.

Mrs. Fielden thinks she is the only person in the world who can make up a fire. And she is perfectly right. She arranged the logs with a long brass poker, shifting them here and there, while her dear face glowed in the light of the fire. She is not a luxurious woman, in spite of being surrounded always by luxury. For instance, she stands and walks in a very erect way, and I have never seen her stuff a lot of sofa cushions at her back in a chair, nor lounge on a sofa. Her glorious, buoyant health seems to exempt her from need of support or ease, and her figure is too pretty for lounging.

When she had finished arranging the logs, she put down the poker and looked at me with that dear kindliness of hers, and said, in her pretty voice: 'What have you been doing with yourself this afternoon?'

'The minister and Evan Sinclair came up to say good-bye,' I said.

'And since then?'

I took my diary, which still lay on my knee, and hid it under the sofa cushions.

'Since then,' I said, 'I have been correcting—that is, writing my diary.'

'Oh, the diary!' exclaimed Mrs. Fielden delightedly. 'I had forgotten about that!'

'No, you hadn't,' I said to myself. 'It is only part of your wilful, uncomprehendable, untranslatable charm that makes you pretend sometimes that you have no memory. As a matter of fact, you knew from the first that it would be a relief to an egotistical grumbler to get rid of his spleen sometimes, on blue ruled essay paper, and so you set him the task to do, and you have often wondered since how he is getting on with it.

'I think I must see the diary,' said Mrs. Fielden.

'That you certainly shall not,' I said; and I pushed the book still farther under the sofa cushions—just as if it were necessary to fight with Mrs. Fielden for anything, or any use either!

'I thought you promised,' said Mrs. Fielden.

'If I did, I have changed my mind,' I said firmly.

'You know you mean all the time to let me see it,' said Mrs. Fielden.

'I know I do not mean to let you see it for even a minute of time,' I replied.

One of Mrs. Fielden's special odd little silences fell between us. 'No,' I said to myself. 'I will *not* say I am sorry. I will *not* say I have been a brute. I will *not* feel a desire to comfort her, even if her eyes take the wistful look upon them.'

Mrs. Fielden sat still and looked into the fire.

What unexpected thing will she do next, I wonder? Will she suddenly burst out laughing, or will she turn and take every bit of manhood out of me by smiling? Or shall I find, when I turn and look at her face, simply that she has gone to sleep?

Good heavens! What if she should be crying? In an agony of compunction I turned and looked at her; and Mrs. Fielden not only smiled, but held out her hand for the book. . . . I rummaged underneath the sofa cushions, and passed it over to her. She bent forward till the firelight from the blazing logs fell full on the open page, and she read every one of those corrected lines. She saw where I had once put 'affected' I had now put 'beautiful,' and for frivolous' I put a 'lovely gaiety,' and she read till she came to the last correction of all. I had run aline through the words 'Mrs. Fielden came to sitwith me,' and had written over it, 'My darling came to see me—' Then Mrs. Fielden closed the book, and left her chair where she had been sitting. She crossed the hearthrug quite slowly till she reached my sofa. And then she kneeled down and took both my hands in her dear strong ones, and looked at me with misty blue eyes, like wet forget-me-nots. 'But Hugo, dear,' she said, 'why did you not tell me so long ago?'

The Codes Of Hammurabi And Moses
W. W. Davies

QTY

The discovery of the Hammurabi Code is one of the greatest achievements of archaeology, and is of paramount interest, not only to the student of the Bible, but also to all those interested in ancient history...

Religion   **ISBN:** *1-59462-338-4*   Pages:132

MSRP $12.95

The Theory of Moral Sentiments
Adam Smith

QTY

This work from 1749. contains original theories of conscience amd moral judgment and it is the foundation for systemof morals.

Philosophy ISBN: *1-59462-777-0*   Pages:536

MSRP $19.95

Jessica's First Prayer
Hesba Stretton

QTY

In a screened and secluded corner of one of the many railway-bridges which span the streets of London there could be seen a few years ago, from five o'clock every morning until half past eight, a tidily set-out coffee-stall, consisting of a trestle and board, upon which stood two large tin cans, with a small fire of charcoal burning under each so as to keep the coffee boiling during the early hours of the morning when the work-people were thronging into the city on their way to their daily toil...

Childrens   ISBN: *1-59462-373-2*   Pages:84

MSRP $9.95

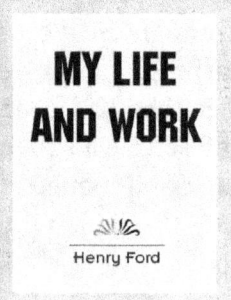

My Life and Work
Henry Ford

QTY

Henry Ford revolutionized the world with his implementation of mass production for the Model T automobile. Gain valuable business insight into his life and work with his own auto-biography... "We have only started on our development of our country we have not as yet, with all our talk of wonderful progress, done more than scratch the surface. The progress has been wonderful enough but..."

Biographies/   ISBN: *1-59462-198-5*   Pages:300

MSRP $21.95

The Art of Cross-Examination
Francis Wellman

QTY

I presume it is the experience of every author, after his first book is published upon an important subject, to be almost overwhelmed with a wealth of ideas and illustrations which could readily have been included in his book, and which to his own mind, at least, seem to make a second edition inevitable. Such certainly was the case with me; and when the first edition had reached its sixth impression in five months, I rejoiced to learn that it seemed to my publishers that the book had met with a sufficiently favorable reception to justify a second and considerably enlarged edition. ..

Reference   ISBN: *1-59462-647-2*

Pages:412

MSRP $19.95

On the Duty of Civil Disobedience
Henry David Thoreau

QTY

Thoreau wrote his famous essay, On the Duty of Civil Disobedience, as a protest against an unjust but popular war and the immoral but popular institution of slave-owning. He did more than write—he declined to pay his taxes, and was hauled off to gaol in consequence. Who can say how much this refusal of his hastened the end of the war and of slavery ?

Law   ISBN: *1-59462-747-9*

Pages:48

MSRP $7.45

Dream Psychology Psychoanalysis for Beginners
Sigmund Freud

QTY

Sigmund Freud, born Sigismund Schlomo Freud (May 6, 1856 - September 23, 1939), was a Jewish-Austrian neurologist and psychiatrist who co-founded the psychoanalytic school of psychology. Freud is best known for his theories of the unconscious mind, especially involving the mechanism of repression; his redefinition of sexual desire as mobile and directed towards a wide variety of objects; and his therapeutic techniques, especially his understanding of transference in the therapeutic relationship and the presumed value of dreams as sources of insight into unconscious desires.

Psychology   ISBN: *1-59462-905-6*

Pages:196

MSRP $15.45

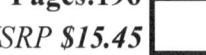

The Miracle of Right Thought
Orison Swett Marden

QTY

Believe with all of your heart that you will do what you were made to do. When the mind has once formed the habit of holding cheerful, happy, prosperous pictures, it will not be easy to form the opposite habit. It does not matter how improbable or how far away this realization may see, or how dark the prospects may be, if we visualize them as best we can, as vividly as possible, hold tenaciously to them and vigorously struggle to attain them, they will gradually become actualized, realized in the life. But a desire, a longing without endeavor, a yearning abandoned or held indifferently will vanish without realization.

Self Help   ISBN: *1-59462-644-8*

Pages:360

MSRP $25.45

QTY

The Rosicrucian Cosmo-Conception Mystic Christianity *by Max Heindel*   ISBN: *1-59462-188-8*   **$38.95**
The Rosicrucian Cosmo-conception is not dogmatic, neither does it appeal to any other authority than the reason of the student. It is: not controversial, but is: sent forth in the, hope that it may help to clear...   New Age/Religion Pages 646

Abandonment To Divine Providence *by Jean-Pierre de Caussade*   ISBN: *1-59462-228-0*   **$25.95**
"The Rev. Jean Pierre de Caussade was one of the most remarkable spiritual writers of the Society of Jesus in France in the 18th Century. His death took place at Toulouse in 1751. His works have gone through many editions and have been republished...   Inspirational/Religion Pages 400

Mental Chemistry *by Charles Haanel*   ISBN: *1-59462-192-6*   **$23.95**
Mental Chemistry allows the change of material conditions by combining and appropriately utilizing the power of the mind. Much like applied chemistry creates something new and unique out of careful combinations of chemicals the mastery of mental chemistry...   New Age Pages 354

The Letters of Robert Browning and Elizabeth Barret Barrett 1845-1846 vol II   ISBN: *1-59462-193-4*   **$35.95**
by Robert Browning and Elizabeth Barrett   Biographies Pages 596

Gleanings In Genesis (volume I) *by Arthur W. Pink*   ISBN: *1-59462-130-6*   **$27.45**
Appropriately has Genesis been termed "the seed plot of the Bible" for in it we have, in germ form, almost all of the great doctrines which are afterwards fully developed in the books of Scripture which follow...   Religion/Inspirational Pages 420

The Master Key *by L. W. de Laurence*   ISBN: *1-59462-001-6*   **$30.95**
In no branch of human knowledge has there been a more lively increase of the spirit of research during the past few years than in the study of Psychology, Concentration and Mental Discipline. The requests for authentic lessons in Thought Control, Mental Discipline and...   New Age/Business Pages 422

The Lesser Key Of Solomon Goetia *by L. W. de Laurence*   ISBN: *1-59462-092-X*   **$9.95**
This translation of the first book of the "Lernegton" which is now for the first time made accessible to students of Talismanic Magic was done, after careful collation and edition, from numerous Ancient Manuscripts in Hebrew, Latin, and French...   New Age/Occult Pages 92

Rubaiyat Of Omar Khayyam *by Edward Fitzgerald*   ISBN: *1-59462-332-5*   **$13.95**
Edward Fitzgerald, whom the world has already learned, in spite of his own efforts to remain within the shadow of anonymity, to look upon as one of the rarest poets of the century, was born at Bredfield, in Suffolk, on the 31st of March, 1809. He was the third son of John Purcell...   Music Pages 172

Ancient Law *by Henry Maine*   ISBN: *1-59462-128-4*   **$29.95**
The chief object of the following pages is to indicate some of the earliest ideas of mankind, as they are reflected in Ancient Law, and to point out the relation of those ideas to modern thought.   Religion/History Pages 452

Far-Away Stories *by William J. Locke*   ISBN: *1-59462-129-2*   **$19.45**
"Good wine needs no bush, but a collection of mixed vintages does. And this book is just such a collection. Some of the stories I do not want to remain buried for ever in the museum files of dead magazine-numbers an author's not unpardonable vanity..."   Fiction Pages 272

Life of David Crockett *by David Crockett*   ISBN: *1-59462-250-7*   **$27.45**
"Colonel David Crockett was one of the most remarkable men of the times in which he lived. Born in humble life, but gifted with a strong will, an indomitable courage, and unremitting perseverance...   Biographies/New Age Pages 424

Lip-Reading *by Edward Nitchie*   ISBN: *1-59462-206-X*   **$25.95**
Edward B. Nitchie, founder of the New York School for the Hard of Hearing, now the Nitchie School of Lip-Reading, Inc, wrote "LIP-READING Principles and Practice". The development and perfecting of this meritorious work on lip-reading was an undertaking...   How-to Pages 400

A Handbook of Suggestive Therapeutics, Applied Hypnotism, Psychic Science   ISBN: *1-59462-214-0*   **$24.95**
by Henry Munro   Health/New Age/Health/Self-help Pages 376

A Doll's House: and Two Other Plays *by Henrik Ibsen*   ISBN: *1-59462-112-8*   **$19.95**
Henrik Ibsen created this classic when in revolutionary 1848 Rome. Introducing some striking concepts in playwriting for the realist genre, this play has been studied the world over.   Fiction/Classics/Plays 308

The Light of Asia *by sir Edwin Arnold*   ISBN: *1-59462-204-3*   **$13.95**
In this poetic masterpiece, Edwin Arnold describes the life and teachings of Buddha. The man who was to become known as Buddha to the world was born as Prince Gautama of India but he rejected the worldly riches and abandoned the reigns of power when...   Religion/History/Biographies Pages 170

The Complete Works of Guy de Maupassant *by Guy de Maupassant*   ISBN: *1-59462-157-8*   **$16.95**
"For days and days, nights and nights, I had dreamed of that first kiss which was to consecrate our engagement, and I knew not on what spot I should put my lips..."   Fiction/Classics Pages 240

The Art of Cross-Examination *by Francis L. Wellman*   ISBN: *1-59462-309-0*   **$26.95**
Written by a renowned trial lawyer, Wellman imparts his experience and uses case studies to explain how to use psychology to extract desired information through questioning.   How-to/Science/Reference Pages 408

Answered or Unanswered? *by Louisa Vaughan*   ISBN: *1-59462-248-5*   **$10.95**
Miracles of Faith in China   Religion Pages 112

The Edinburgh Lectures on Mental Science (1909) *by Thomas*   ISBN: *1-59462-008-3*   **$11.95**
This book contains the substance of a course of lectures recently given by the writer in the Queen Street Hall, Edinburgh. Its purpose is to indicate the Natural Principles governing the relation between Mental Action and Material Conditions...   New Age/Psychology Pages 148

Ayesha *by H. Rider Haggard*   ISBN: *1-59462-301-5*   **$24.95**
Verily and indeed it is the unexpected that happens! Probably if there was one person upon the earth from whom the Editor of this, and of a certain previous history, did not expect to hear again...   Classics Pages 380

Ayala's Angel *by Anthony Trollope*   ISBN: *1-59462-352-X*   **$29.95**
The two girls were both pretty, but Lucy who was twenty-one who supposed to be simple and comparatively unattractive, whereas Ayala was credited, as her Bombwhat romantic name might show, with poetic charm and a taste for romance. Ayala when her father died was nineteen...   Fiction Pages 484

The American Commonwealth *by James Bryce*   ISBN: *1-59462-286-8*   **$34.45**
An interpretation of American democratic political theory. It examines political mechanics and society from the perspective of Scotsman James Bryce   Politics Pages 572

Stories of the Pilgrims *by Margaret P. Pumphrey*   ISBN: *1-59462-116-0*   **$17.95**
This book explores pilgrims religious oppression in England as well as their escape to Holland and eventual crossing to America on the Mayflower, and their early days in New England...   History Pages 268

QTY

The Fasting Cure *by Sinclair Upton*   ISBN: *1-59462-222-1*   **$13.95**
In the Cosmopolitan Magazine for May, 1910, and in the Contemporary Review (London) for April, 1910, I published an article dealing with my experiences in fasting. I have written a great many magazine articles, but never one which attracted so much attention...   New Age/Self Help/Health Pages 164

Hebrew Astrology *by Sepharial*   ISBN: *1-59462-308-2*   **$13.45**
In these days of advanced thinking it is a matter of common observation that we have left many of the old landmarks behind and that we are now pressing forward to greater heights and to a wider horizon than that which represented the mind-content of our progenitors...   Astrology Pages 144

Thought Vibration or The Law of Attraction in the Thought World   ISBN: *1-59462-127-6*   **$12.95**
by William Walker Atkinson   *Psychology/Religion Pages 144*

Optimism *by Helen Keller*   ISBN: *1-59462-108-X*   **$15.95**
Helen Keller was blind, deaf, and mute since 19 months old, yet famously learned how to overcome these handicaps, communicate with the world, and spread her lectures promoting optimism. An inspiring read for everyone...   Biographies/Inspirational Pages 84

Sara Crewe *by Frances Burnett*   ISBN: *1-59462-360-0*   **$9.45**
In the first place, Miss Minchin lived in London. Her home was a large, dull, tall one, in a large, dull square, where all the houses were alike, and all the sparrows were alike, and where all the door-knockers made the same heavy sound...   Childrens/Classic Pages 88

The Autobiography of Benjamin Franklin *by Benjamin Franklin*   ISBN: *1-59462-135-7*   **$24.95**
The Autobiography of Benjamin Franklin has probably been more extensively read than any other American historical work, and no other book of its kind has had such ups and downs of fortune. Franklin lived for many years in England, where he was agent...   Biographies/History Pages 332

Name	
Email	
Telephone	
Address	
City, State ZIP	

☐ **Credit Card**   ☐ **Check / Money Order**

Credit Card Number	
Expiration Date	
Signature	

Please Mail to: Book Jungle
PO Box 2226
Champaign, IL 61825
or Fax to: 630-214-0564

ORDERING INFORMATION

web*: www.bookjungle.com*
email*: sales@bookjungle.com*
fax*: 630-214-0564*
mail*: Book Jungle PO Box 2226 Champaign, IL 61825*
or PayPal *to sales@bookjungle.com*

Please contact us for bulk discounts

DIRECT-ORDER TERMS

20% Discount if You Order
Two or More Books
Free Domestic Shipping!
Accepted: Master Card, Visa,
Discover, American Express